Dead Horse Bay

John Dyson

Mighty Hamster Press
Brooklyn, New York

ISBN 978-0-578-87757-0

Library of Congress Control Number: 2021905443

Cover Illustration by Alex Foster

Edited by Tim M. Hawley (HAWLEY WORD STUDIO)

Mighty Hamster Press
Brooklyn, New York

Forest Park
Brooklyn
Queens
Prospect Park
Spring Creek
JFK International Airport
Green-Wood Cemetary
Owls Head Park/ Shore Road
Wildlife Refuge
Marine Park/ Gerritsen Creek
Floyd Bennett Field
Dead Horse Bay
Arverne Piping Plover Site
Riis Park
Breezy Point
Fort Tilden

Contents

PART ONE

2.   DEAD HORSE BAY

Duck, Duck, Goose

Duck, Duck, Goose: A traditional children's game that originated in Sweden.

It was early June and the bus was loaded with people heading out from the city to the Rockaway Beaches at the southern tip of Brooklyn, and Marty knew he was lucky to have a seat. Turning to look out of the nearest window, he watched the wire railings along Mill Basin Inlet holding up the plastic bags pinned to them by the prevailing south wind. Looking ahead, he noticed that nobody on the bus was watching the sunrise as the first rays of the sun appeared over the water. He got off the bus at Gateway Marina, which catered to the car-owning affluent, so he was the only passenger who departed there.

Marty hadn't brought much with him. He packed a sandwich for lunch, a jar of marine grease, and he'd also remembered to bring a spoon and some cans of cat food for the marina's cats.

His destination was his boat. Gateway Marina was in Dead Horse Bay. From where he stood, a narrow beach formed the left side of the bay; it led to the Rockaway Inlet. Windrows of debris formed lines along the beach, and in the distance he could easily see many large, rust-colored shells of dead horseshoe crabs.

On Marty's right, the dark sand beach led to Gerritsen Inlet, where tall, reeds grew to 10 or 11 feet and framed the beach. Old growth towered over the freshly sprouted green reeds. The reeds had hollow stalks an inch thick and left no room for any other plant. In the summer, each reed had small reddish flowers that provided food for the large broadwinged skipper butterflies that stopped off in the bay. The reeds had long, sharp, bluish-green leaves, and green stems with spots of yellow.

4.   DEAD HORSE BAY

The sun reflected off the ripples in the water of the bay and overcame the surroundings of noise, dirt, and trash. In many ways, it was like every other bay except that the beach on the left was awash with broken bottles, gifts from the landfill that washed out from where the cap on the landfill had broken. Marty was old enough to have seen this happen.

The bay earned its name because of the dead horses that New York City had dumped there in the 1800s to be processed for glue and fertilizer. The beach on the left was known to locals as Bottle Beach. The area had been the site of several horse rendering plants, and horse bones along with the bottles that washed out of the landfill and littered the beach. The place had a history, and Marty felt that reverence was due to the bones and the bottles of Bottle Beach.

Marty walked towards the water, six foot two inches tall and gangly at 73 years old, he watched his reflection in the windows as he passed the three blue sheds that had been connected and labeled as "Buster's Marine." The blue of the sheds stood out from the blue sky and the blue sea; it was a shade of blue that people who liked blues would not like. The fourth shed was black. It had once been a café and was boarded up. It was a shame, really, because inside Buster's there was little to eat, and it took a real effort to get Buster to make fresh coffee. A National Park Service sign had been nailed to Buster's; it read: "The feeding of wildlife, feral cats and dogs is not permitted." Underneath the sign were three empty cat bowls.

Marty filled the bowls with the cat food that he had brought. He waited for the cats, but they stood off at a distance. There were six cats in all, a family of four thin black cats and two small gray ones who looked to be wary of each other. He concluded that they would not approach while he remained there, so he entered Buster's store and watched the cat bowls through the window in the door. The cats approached timidly, and Marty happily watched them eat until Cathy, who worked at Buster's, came up behind him, "The cats mostly eat ducklings, and ducklings are better for cats than tinned cat food. Ducklings have roughage and no additives," she said.

"Can't you stop the cats from eating ducklings?" Marty asked.

"Cats have always eaten ducklings. I put out food for the cats but the cats still eat the ducks," said Cathy, whose skin and yellow teeth revealed a decades-long cigarette habit.

"Don't you feel bad for the ducks?"

"There isn't a duck aisle at Petco. Cats have personality, ducks don't."

Marty saw her catch herself as she stumbled on the uneven floor before he asked, "Are you okay?"

"I have good days and bad days. Today is a good day, but no matter what day it is, nobody pays any attention to me," Cathy replied.

"I'm sorry to hear that," Marty said as he headed out of the store.

Cathy looked unhappy with his response. Marty hesitated at the door, realizing that this was the first time she had articulated her feelings. She had expected more, but Marty knew that if he did not move on, he would spend most of the day listening to her tales of woe.

Walking down the ramp that led to the floating dock, he turned left and fell into his regular habit of observing the wind, the sky, and the water. He was a sailor at heart. The place had the familiar smell of salt and seaweed, and in the background he heard seagulls fighting over food. The wind shifted, carrying the mixed scent of diesel fuel and the dead fish that were floating and bouncing against the dock. Marty put on his sunglasses, mostly to shield his eyes from the sun's glare and reflections, but also to isolate himself a little.

His boat was a Skipper 20 that he called Soft Kitty, a squat, chubby, double-ended sailboat, made in England in 1979. The boat had a plastic hull, but it was molded as though it were made from wood planks, and people who didn't know better thought it was made of wood. He had owned the boat for 20 years, longer than all his friendships. The sails were worn out; he couldn't pull them into shape and didn't have the cash to replace them. One of the sail-handling cleats was loose; a nail and a cardboard wedge tenuously held it in place.

Several minutes later, Marty was watching the sun rise higher when he saw a young woman coming his way. As she approached, he saw that she had a badge pinned to her shirt. When she got close enough, he saw that the message on the badge read: "Save the Geese." She was small and dark-skinned, with bright white eyes and dark brown irises. Her shoulders were tanned almost black. She was slim, and her prominent shoulder-bones gave her a somewhat frail appearance. She was wearing a sleeveless orange shirt, red pants, and what looked like an expensive watch. She looked like she would talk through a smile, unlike other visitors to Dead Horse Bay who were a little glum.

"Hi," she said, eyeing the empty cat food cans that were still next to Marty. And then she asked, "Are you an animal lover?"

"I used to like cats, but I went off them just this morning when Cathy at Buster's Marine said that they ate ducklings," Marty replied.

"Do you have a cat?" she asked, looking concerned.

"I had a cat but it ran off." He then asked, "What's your name?"

"Tanisha. I'm a student at Brooklyn Law School." She noticed Marty staring at her badge and asked, "Can you help me save the geese?"

"Nobody's bothering the geese. The cats eat ducklings."

"Cats also eat goslings, but that's not the problem."

"What is the problem?"

"A plane collided with a flock of geese. There is a plan to kill all of the geese near the airport."

"That was over a year ago."

"Yes, they killed the geese in Prospect Park last month and they plan to kill the geese at the airport next."

"Do they shoot the geese?"

With tears rolling down her cheeks, Tanisha replied, "No, they wait until they molt and cannot fly, and then they catch them, crate them, and ship them away to be gassed."

Marty knew about the collision. There was a picture of a plane that had landed in the Hudson River on the front page of the newspaper. Marty was a birdwatcher, but he didn't think that geese were beautiful birds. His favorite bird was the yellow warbler—the first bird he ever identified. It had a bright, sweet song and it was the first bird that he heard most springs. He figured that geese might not be popular right now, but he agreed with Tanisha. They should not kill the geese.

"I heard about the collision. Captain Sully is a hero. He ditched his plane in the Hudson River and nobody got hurt," Marty replied.

"You have a boat. You could get me to the airport."

"Which airport?"

"Kennedy."

"But didn't Sully take off from LaGuardia?"

"They plan to kill all the geese that live close to airports, and geese breed near Kennedy."

"And what do we do when we get there?"

"I could document the goose roundup."

"How?"

"By keeping count of the geese and taking video of the roundup as they crate the geese and carry them away."

"Why?"

"It will draw attention and maybe stop the round-up."

"Documenting the round-up won't save the geese."

"It might. Can you take me out there please?"

"I need to think. Can you come back later?"

"Yes, I'll come back," Tanisha replied.

Marty had only ever noticed geese in winter, when there was nothing alive in Dead Horse Bay except for them. Last winter, one time when he checked on his boat, he took shelter from the wind to warm up. He was watching the sky when first he heard and then saw the geese. They came in from the east and made a black silhouette against the gray sky, showing off an infinite variety of flying V formations. After he heard them, there was a persistent quack-quack, like a duck, but the sound was deeper. As the wind increased, they settled into a long V formation, one goose leading and the rest two abreast as they flew into it. At one point, he had thought that they were flying in family groups. Their necks were not quite horizontal, a little lower at the front, and Marty was fascinated by the small, up-and-down neck movements they made as they flew. It was as if they were moving their necks to keep their heads level. Occasionally the leader fell back into one of the arms of the V and another, from the first echelon, took the leader's place and gave the leader a rest from having to break the wind. Toward the end of the display, they did a roll, each goose rolling in perfect order.

He did feel bad for the geese. His ex-wife had always thought of him as an old softy, a sucker for a cause. But could he go in with Tanisha? She seemed genuine, if a little over-involved, and maybe she had a bigger agenda. No one else he knew at the marina was concerned about the goose kill, but wasn't it always the case that righteous causes draw only a little support?

Marty needed to talk to someone before Tanisha came back to get an opinion about her request for help. It was midweek and the marina was pretty much deserted. There was Ed in the yard who never said much and some Polish sailors on his dock with whom he'd exchanged greetings and smiles. There was Cathy at Buster's. Marty didn't see her as being knowledgeable, but she was nosy and she did watch most of the goings-on at the marina. This might make up for it.

Retracing his way up the dock, Marty realized he wasn't very keen to talk with Cathy. She'd looked at him accusingly when he left her without inquiring about her illness, but she was still there, behind the store counter when he got back.

"Do you know anything about Tanisha?" Marty asked.

"I talked to her about cats," Cathy replied.

"Yes, but what's she like?" Marty said.

"She likes cats and she understands them. Her husband has a boat on J dock. He works out at Kennedy," Cathy said.

"She's asking me to take her out to the airport so that she can help geese."

"You have to be careful. There was a kayaker who got lost near the airport. He ended up wandering onto one of the runways and was arrested."

"Should I help her?"

"She likes cats. You should help her. Just be careful, and don't get lost."

"But …"

"Gotta go. Unlike you, I have work to do," as she turned to straighten some cans on her shelf.

Marty returned to his boat and sat down on the dock.

When Tanisha returned, Marty offered her a share of his lunch before they started their conversation. She ate eagerly, saying that she had skipped breakfast.

"Did you ask anyone else for help rescuing the geese?" Marty asked.

"Yes, but they said no," Tanisha replied.

"Can't your husband take you out to the airport? He has a boat."

"How do you know about my husband?"

"I talked to Cathy at the store."

"How does she know that he has a boat?" Tanisha said.

"Cathy sold him some boat supplies last week. She also told me about a guy who got lost near the airport and got arrested," Marty said.

"My husband can't go. Someone would recognize him. He works at the airport and would lose his job if he were seen. You know, in my neighborhood it's tough to get help. Most people don't have the time. But there is this sweet lady called Sally who lives on my block who has turned her front yard into an educational center. There's a sunshade in the center, and to the front there are panels that she's covered with dot patterns sprayed on with Rust-Oleum paint, and she claims that she uses these to teach multiplication. To the left of the sunshade, there is an old mop covered with molding flour, which she says she uses to teach bacteria growth. To the right, there's a can full of dirty water that she left in the sun to teach the creation of life. She says that God created the universe from dirty water, and she offered to help me educate people about geese, but she can't get me out to the airport," Tanisha replied.

"Most people don't have sympathy for the geese."

"I can't get out there. The area near the airport where the geese are is inaccessible except by boat."

"Maybe I'll take you," Marty said, "but not today."

"You mean it?"

"Maybe, but some other time," he said, glancing down at his feet.

"Can I call you? I need to know for sure."

"If we go out on my boat, I'll be in charge."

"It's just a small boat."

"It's my small boat. I'm in charge."

"So, can I call you? I know that you'll get me out there safely."

And to his surprise, Marty replied "Yes." He took out a pen and a small slip of paper and wrote his phone number on it. She looked at the paper, carefully folded it, and put it in her back pants pocket before she headed down the dock.

Marty had lived in Brooklyn all his life. Having grown up there, he could remember the way the bay was before the airport was constructed. During the Second World War, his mother and father owned a café near

Canarsie Pier, and he'd spent a lot of time there helping his father when he was a boy. He saw how airport construction had ruined the bay. He was 10 years old when his childhood playground, the marsh, was dredged for the landfill necessary to build the airport. The dredging turned the marsh, which was once full of life, into a dead zone. There were borrow pits, dredged to a depth of 50 feet, for the landfill needed to construct the airport. There was a huge dredger with a huge bucket, and huge barges carried the sand away. The deep holes sucked up the plankton, the oxygen, and the life from the water.

Once the airport opened, the noise of jet engines messed with his sleep. He'd gone to school in Canarsie, where the noise had also messed with his schooling. The jets' noise drowned out his teachers' voices until one-by-one they had all adapted to the noise with "jet-pause teaching."

At first, Marty thought that crews would eventually fill in the borrow pits and restore the marshland. The name, "borrow pit," said to him that the sand was borrowed and would be put back, but he was disappointed. A new barge did appear three years after they had dug the pits, but it was empty. They were not going to fill in the borrow pits; the barge was just for another round of dredging.

Jibe-Oh!

For Marty, mornings were best because his leg did not bother him early in the day. His favorite meal was breakfast with eggs and decaf coffee, and on this particular morning he was up early to meet with Tanisha; they were going to sail from Dead Horse Bay to the marshland near Kennedy airport and rescue the geese.

The weather was cool for June, and Marty was wearing layers, four layers to be exact, as he waited by his boat for Tanisha to turn up at his slip on J dock. Tanisha was late, but Marty was pleased that she was wearing black pants and a dark windbreaker for the trip. Her dark clothes would help her to go undetected when they went ashore at night.

"What are you wearing?" Tanisha asked as she laughed.

"I got the jacket at a thrift store. I have on four top layers and two pairs of pants," Marty replied.

"You are a fashion statement," she said, continuing to laugh.

Marty's routine for departing from the dock was careful, neat, and tidy. He stowed the boat covers, and he coiled the ropes. He turned the boat in the slip so that he could leave bow first.

Apart from the cool breeze, the weather for the trip was good. Marty noticed that the wind was from the southwest and shifty—it was too early in the season for the summer south-wind pattern to set in. The tide was at low water plus one hour; it would soon be coming in rapidly, and there would be a helpful current once they were in the channel. The sky was mostly clear with high-flying cumulus clouds, signaling fair weather. If the weather turned foul after they passed under the Marine Parkway Bridge, there were plenty of places to shelter.

Once clear of the marina, Marty followed the breakwater using the motor.

"Why can't we sail straight to the bridge?" Tanisha asked.

"There's a sandbank to our left, and if there wasn't the sandbank, we still couldn't sail direct. We have to dog-leg it," Marty replied.

Marty turned east at the end of the breakwater, and after rounding buoy nine, he cut the engine and hoisted the mainsail. Gripping the tiller as the sail filled, he set out on a beam reach (the wind is blowing over the boat at a 90 degree angle) towards the bridge. Marty enjoyed sailing, but today he was tense, he could not get into it. He was with a companion whom he hardly knew and heading toward an airport that scared him.

"We're barely moving. Can you speed up?" Tanisha said.

"It's a sailboat," Marty replied.

"It will take us all day to get to the airport," Tanisha said.

"We will get to the airport before dark," Marty replied.

Marty then handed Tanisha a life vest and said," Put this on."

"I can swim," Tanisha replied.

"You must put it on for safety. In June, the water is still cold and you will suffer from hypothermia if you fall in," Marty said.

Tanisha put the life vest on and this satisfied Marty.

"Tell me something about yourself," Marty asked.

"I never see my husband. I live in downtown Brooklyn with my step-mother and I don't care for her. My sister lives in England and I miss her. I am not happy here. I want to move away." Marty started to sympathize and smiled as she continued, "I like the name Dead Horse Bay, it suits my mood. I have a poem I wrote called 'Death.' I like the death theme, but I have to be back home by tomorrow afternoon when my husband gets back," Tanisha said.

Marty looked puzzled, "It doesn't make sense," he said.

"What doesn't?" Tanisha replied,

"You said that you don't see your husband anymore, but that you had to be back before he gets back," Marty said.

"I did? It might be wishful thinking," Tanisha said.

"You did, and you're not looking at me when you talk."

"He doesn't pay attention to me anymore. He's more interested in his job at the airport."

"What does he do?"

"He's a security guard."

"But you do see him sometimes. I'm confused," Marty said.

"Well at least I'm not a hypocrite," Tanisha replied.

"What do you mean?"

"You told me to put on this life vest but you are not wearing one. You put yourself in the danger that you warned me about."

"I never wear a life vest. Never have and never will."

"Why?"

"It's better to drown straight away than to float around for hours and then drown. Like if you catch a fish, kill it. Don't let it die slowly from lack of breath."

"Let's call a truce. Neither of us is perfect. Let's not argue. It's a nice day," Tanisha said.

Marty saw the logic to this and he shut up.

The first part of the dog-leg took them out to buoys nine and ten in Dead Horse Bay. In the second part, Marty headed south, parallel to the shore and about 200 yards out from Dead Horse Bay when Tanisha pointed to the beach and asked, "Do you know anything about the bottles that are washed up on the beach? Do you think any of them have messages in them?"

"The bottles were washed out of the ground. There are no messages in them. There is no romance. Nobody threw the bottles overboard in a search for romance like the character in the Nicholas Sparks novel.

"The dunes that you see are on the landfill that was capped, but a storm broke through the cap. They dredged to build the airport and dug 80-foot holes in the Rockaway Inlet, and when those holes filled up again, the trash from the landfill washed into them. I saw it happen summer by summer. I grew up near here," Marty replied.

"Why did they dredge?" Tanisha asked.

"They needed the sediment to extend the land and build the airport," Marty replied.

Marty continued south on a beam reach and then fell off into a channel that led to the Gil Hodges Memorial Marine Park Bridge, one of the three bridges that connect Brooklyn to the Rockaways. The flood tide was running at two knots, and Marty's speed over the ground increased to five. The boat had a distinct wake and ripple as they kept their speed. Marty was pleased with the speed increase, but he relaxed and looked at Tanisha just as the wind shifted 20 degrees.

Marty realized his mistake, but he was late yelling, "Jibe-ho!"

Tanisha ducked as the boom swung violently across the cockpit.

Marty wasn't as quick, but he managed to stand up and turn away from the boom as it came towards him, so as not to get smacked in the face. The boom missed his head but he felt the blow to his shoulders. It was bruisingly painful, and the main sheet—the rope that controlled the boom—caught in the collar of his jacket. Marty was pinned against the cockpit coaming as the boat picked up speed on the opposite tack. Tanisha tried to pull the rope off him but as she pulled the rope the boat changed direction and Marty remained pinned.

"Get it off me! Pull it off me," Marty shouted.

"I could have been hurt," Tanisha said.

"You are okay. Pull the rope off me," Marty replied.

"I can't. The wind is too strong," Tanisha said. And it was only after Marty rolled under the rope and onto the cockpit sole that he managed to free his collar and extract himself. As he stood up, she asked, "Are you hurt?"

"My leg hurts. It's been bothering me," Marty replied. Rising slowly, Marty said, "The air temperature makes a big difference. It makes you clumsy."

Tanisha shivered and looked straight at Marty as she replied, "Yeah, that and your age." and she went on to say, "You know Marty, if you had gone overboard you would have sunk. You're wearing four layers of clothing and heavy boots. You don't look like you work out at the gym, and once those layers got wet, they would be really heavy."

"I'm glad that you are looking out for me. My mind isn't on sailing, I'm worried about airport security. If they catch us there, we will be arrested. When I was a kid you could explore the airport, but now it is a crime, so we have to be careful not to go inside the airport fence," Marty said.

"But it's worth it. Geese are special. Few events are more exciting to watch than the V formation of Canada geese. I've seen them in the winter when it's really cold. They fly fast, and the males and females honk greetings and signal to each other," Tanisha replied.

As they went under the central span of the Marine Parkway Bridge, the whine of car tires on the metal roadway 50 feet above them disturbed the boat's peaceful gliding. It subsided as they came out on the other side. It was quiet under the middle of the bridge, but then the whine came back as they went under the traffic heading north. Once away from the bridge, they faced fresh obstacles: the wind was dying, and there were several anchored fishing boats ahead. The landscape was also changing as the inlet merged into Jamaica Bay.

Out from under the bridge, Marty continued for a while until he was well clear of it. Then he turned into the wind, dropped the sail, and started the engine. The bridge seemed to be far away and the engine was noisy. Marty shouted a couple of things before he realized that Tanisha couldn't hear him. He then fell silent for the long trip to the second bridge.

They continued motoring in silence under the second bridge, the stone-built Cross Bay Memorial Bridge, and into the East Broad Channel. They continued for another hour, until Marty put the motor in neutral and looked around the bay. Marshlands surrounded them. There were small islands with strange names like Winhole Hassack, Hissock Manor, Yellow Bar Hassock, The Raunt, Jack's Hole, and East High Meadow. There was also Broad Creek Marsh, Broad Channel, and directly ahead, near the airport, a polluted area called Grassy Bay. Marty put the motor back in gear and followed the marker buoys inland in Broad Channel until it opened out into Grassy Bay. Marty then cut the motor and let the boat drift for a few minutes before they dropped anchor in 20 feet of water about 100 yards out from the airport.

With the noisy motor off, Marty said "This is Grassy Bay. This all used to be marsh and tidal channels with salt-marsh cord-grass, salt grass, black grass, and sea lavender. On the water, there were salt marsh skippers and the air was full of butterflies, dragonflies, and damselflies. In the water there were snails, fish, and small crabs, and frogs, toads, newts, and snakes." Marty then pointed inland and west before continuing, "I grew up over there. There was no airport back then." He paused while Tanisha looked about and then said, "The Port Authority calls this part of the bay the dead zone. They claim that nothing grows here and that nothing was harmed here when they dredged to get the material to build aircraft runways."

"They kill the possibility of growth. Do you remember Sally's teaching project? She had a bucket filled with dirty water that came to life," Tanisha replied.

"You said that she was nuts," Marty said.

"She is, but her dirty water did come to life. If you held her container to the light, you could see things moving," Tanisha replied.

"Forget Sally," Marty said.

Marty then picked up a pair of binoculars and began to look over the dead water towards the airport, first scanning the hangers, the terminals, and the tails of the airplanes before he switched his gaze to the airport's perimeter fence. He was looking for a gate, and after he found one, he pointed and said, "Do you see the gate in the fence?"

"Yes, I see some empty crates next to it," Tanisha said, following Marty's arm.

"I have wire cutters. I'll cut holes in the crates," Marty said.

"Are you sure that the crates are for the geese?" Tanisha asked.

"You said that they crate them," Marty replied.

"Are there any geese?"

"I can't see any."

"It's perhaps as well. If you get caught cutting holes in crates, it's a misdemeanor and you will get away with a fine. If you interfere with a goose roundup you might end up in jail. Some animal liberation activists have been tried for eco-terrorism, and they went to jail."

"I also see something on a trailer, it's big, could be a truck or it could be a boat. I can't make it out. It's like nothing that I have seen before. Get the hand bearing compass, and I'll get a compass bearing to the gate in the airport fence before it gets dark. We can use the bearing when we go ashore after dark."

The Airport at Night

Marty waited until it was almost dark and then put on an extra layer of clothes before going ashore. He made no noise as he took the boat in closer to shore and rolled up his pants legs before stepping off the boat and into the water. The water was cold. He carried a compass, a pocket knife, a flashlight, and some matches; he also had a hammer and some wire cutters stuffed in his belt. Tanisha carried a flashlight, but she didn't have it turned on.

Following close behind him, Tanisha asked "Why did you bring the hammer?"

"Not sure, I brought a few tools," Marty replied.

Marty had taken his shoes off, and after the small beach he felt grass and small stones underneath his feet. Some of the small stones had sharp edges, so he put his shoes back on. There were fireflies, gnats, and moths visible against the skyline, as was the airport fence.

Marty then looked up, saying, "It's dark here, I wish there was a moon."

"There is, it's a crescent moon."

"Well, it's not helping. Shine the flashlight over here. It looks like there's a path that goes inland. Let's see if it leads to the gate."

Marty then took the flashlight from Tanisha, and with the light he slowly made his way inland. At the fence, he stopped and looked through it toward the distant aircraft hangers, some airplanes, and the empty runway. The airport looked like a prison with razor wire topping its chain-link fence and perimeter lights. He noticed the humming of engines coming from the airport and the quiet of the marsh behind him before he said, "I don't see any geese."

Tanisha stopped next to him and replied, "They may be out on the water. They might have gone for a swim."

"Didn't your husband see geese out here?" Marty replied.

"Yes, he did. He said he saw a lot of them but that they were not molting and not in danger of being rounded up," said Tanisha.

"Shall we go left or right?" Marty asked.

"Can't you follow your compass bearing?"

"I did, but I had to follow the path and it didn't go in a straight line. Let's go a hundred yards to the right, and if we don't find the gate we'll turn back," Marty replied. He then began to count off his paces as he followed the fence. He passed a few no-trespassing signs affixed to the airport fence, then, at 23 paces he saw a large, plastic-wrapped paper sign tied to the fence. It began, "Please don't feed waterfowl."

Please don't feed waterfowl. Regular feeding of waterfowl can cause:

- Poor nutrition
- Pollution
- Spread of disease
- Overcrowding
- Unnatural behavior
- Delayed migration

Many people enjoy feeding waterfowl, but the effects of this seemingly generous act can be harmful. If you care about waterfowl, please stop feeding them.

"Why is the notice posted here? Nobody comes here," Tanisha asked.

"There aren't any geese to feed, but we should still pay attention to the notice," Marty replied. "We won't feed the geese," he added with a sarcastic tone.

Marty then lit a match and was about to set the notice alight when Tanisha interrupted him.

"Are you crazy? Someone might see the fire!"

"What is unnatural behavior in waterfowl?"

"They might have kinky sex or start to moo."

Marty laughed and then said, "It's a stupid sign." He pulled it down, balled it up, and threw it over the fence.

Tanisha grabbed Marty's arm and pointed through the fence and said, "Do you see the guard shining his flashlight as if he's looking for something? Get down. It looks like he works for Ace Security."

"How can you tell?"

"The company name is on the truck, and don't you see the four red balls above the name? It's the logo. Don't move until he moves away."

"How do you know about the logo?"

"I told you my husband is in security."

"That's not him?"

"No, he works at the desk."

"Does he know anything about the guys who are rounding up the geese?"

"The airport hires the US Fish and Wildlife Service, the USDA, to round up the geese."

"Do you know the names of the people at the USDA?"

"My husband gave me two names from the airport sign-in log. They have to sign in at the security desk when they visit the airport. The guy in charge is Bill Bruford, and his sidekick is Donny. Bill Bruford lives in Howard Beach."

"Wasn't Bill Bruford the drummer for Yes?"

"It's not the same guy. The Yes drummer didn't start a second career rounding up geese."

Marty watched the security guard for several minutes, keeping out of sight all the while. When the security guard got back in the truck and drove off, Marty asked, "Did you notice his limp?"

"Yes, but be more careful. I think that the guard heard you when you pulled down the sign and threw it over the fence," Tanisha replied.

Marty then silently counted 20 steps before he stepped on something soft. Stooping to pick it up, he recoiled somewhat when he realized that he had picked up a dead seagull that had probably been shot because it was near the airport. After another 40 steps, tall reeds blocked his path.

At first he tried to walk through the reeds, but there were too many of them. The grass was nine feet tall and tough, and it grew close together. It blocked his path, making it impossible to squeeze through it. He then turned to go back down to the beach and work his way around it. The beach was soft and Marty could no longer hear Tanisha's footsteps behind him; this made him feel uneasy. Turning, he said, "You blend right into the darkness. I can't hear you."

"I can see pretty well. Switch off your flashlight and you will also see better," said Tanisha, and she grabbed Marty's hand and pulled him back inland to a second path that led to the gate.

The fence was broken near the gate, and Marty stepped forward to check out the opening.

"Don't you remember Sally's warning about the kayaker who got arrested for trespassing at the airport?" Tanisha said.

Marty stepped back smartly. Just then, he spotted the empty bird crates next to the locked gate. He handed the flashlight back to Tanisha and said, "Hold the light on a crate while I test my wire cutters." His wire cutters worked fine and rewarded him with a chink-chink noise as they snapped the wires on the top of the crate. Moving to the side of the cage, Marty then made several cuts to adjacent vertical bars, making a hole wide enough for a goose to escape and making the crate unusable for crating geese. Then, to dispose of the wire that he had cut out, he spun them into the reeds using a backhand throw.

As Marty moved to the second cage, Tanisha said, "Are you sure that you want to do this?"

"The notice said not to feed waterfowl. It didn't say anything about cutting holes in crates," Marty replied.

Ten crates later, Marty stopped cutting holes in the crates and instead tried to flatten them with his hammer. That didn't work; the crates bent a little and then sprang back. He cursed as he cut his hand on one of the pieces of wire and stopped working on the crates.

"You are so methodical, but why don't you take a rest from monkey wrenching?" said Tanisha, as she sat down on one of the intact crates

"I don't have a wrench. I have wire cutters and a hammer," Marty replied.

"Did you ever read *The Monkey Wrench Gang* by Edward Abbey? It's a book about a desert in the southwest that's threatened by industrial development. The Monkey Wrench Gang set fire to billboards and wrecked a bridge and a coal train in their effort to stop the development," Tanisha said.

"I have a copy. I liked the George Hayduke character – I always wanted to act like him," Marty replied.

"But he littered and was an explosives-expert."

"I'm not into explosives."

"'I hope you are not into littering either."

"I might litter, if it makes me look like Hayduke."

"There were other groups who also tried to stop the industrial development in the southwestern desert. There was Earth First! and the Sierra Club. Just like now, Marty, there is Audubon and the group that I belong to called Goose Watch."

"What's Goose Watch?"

"It's a group that I belong to. It's trying to save the geese. You should join."

"I'm not sure that I care for geese. My favorite bird is the yellow warbler."

"They are wonderful creatures. Once you get to know them, you will like them."

"I'm a loner, but I like the sound of Goose Watch better than the sound of the Audubon Society. When the geese vanished from the airport, the Audubon Society claimed that they had suddenly flown off."

"You would also have liked Earth First more than you would have liked the Sierra Club.

Fifteen minutes later, having not taken a rest, Marty sat down next to Tanisha on the one goose crate still intact, and the chink-chink of his wire cutters stopped.

"What do they do with the geese after they crate them?" he asked.

"They take them to a hangar at the airport and they gas them. They then double-bag them and truck them out of the airport. They then get dumped in the landfill."

"Do you know where?"

"No."

Marty then set off again, following the dirt road that exited the airport at the gate, back towards the water. He was curious about the machine that he had seen from his boat and he wanted to take a closer look.

The machine was perhaps 20 yards inland and secured to a trailer. Approaching it cautiously, Tanisha asked, "What is it?"

Marty shone the light on it and replied, "It says deep-clean machine."

"For cleaning what?" Tanisha asked.

"I don't know, but there is a cleat on it."

"What is a cleat?"

Marty reached up and put his hand on a piece of metal that was sticking out of the machine's deck, it had the shape of an anvil. "This is a cleat. You use it to tie a boat to a dock. This is a boat. It's large; it's at least 30 feet long. The launch ramp is by the water," he said.

Marty dimmed the light by covering the lens with a napkin and passed it to Tanisha, saying "Hold the light on it. Someone woke up one morning and dreamed this thing up. I can dream stuff up myself when I don't have a hangover, but I never dreamt of anything like this. There is a 10-foot boom with blades at the end that the crew can lower into the water. You can see marsh grass and reeds on the blades. It's used to cut marsh grass and reeds, but it cuts under the water. It's a floating combined harvester. The grass that's cut then travels up the conveyor belt and onto the chute. I bet they collect the grass from the chute and take it away.

"Shine the light to the side. There's a manufacturer's nameplate that says that it's an aquatic plant harvester. Made by Aquarius Systems, a division of D and D products, North Prairie, Wisconsin. It's driven by paddle wheels. Everything on it is controlled by hydraulics and hydraulic motors. Look at all that hydraulic tubing. There are separate tubes to the paddle wheels, the boom, the conveyor, and the cutting blades."

The whole area lit up as an airplane came in low. Marty heard the noise first and then saw the black silhouette against the moon. There were red and green lights at the end of the wings, a white light on the tail, and really bright landing lights underneath the aircraft. The cabin appeared to be in darkness and the noise of the jet engines was deafening; yet underneath this noise, they heard a low, constant hum and whine.

After the airplane passed overhead, Marty continued, "This is supposed to be part of the Gateway National Park. It's supposed to be park right up to the airport fence. But as soon as the geese threaten the airport, the geese suffer. There is the notice telling us not to feed waterfowl, but they are destroying the bird's food. Their concern is so phony. They don't want the geese fed because they don't want them here.

"They are also using the harvester to cut the vegetation that the geese feed on. They are killing the food supply. The geese eat the low marsh grass, the salt grass, the black grass, and the glasswort and sea lavender, and they are removing it."

Tanisha took a while to take this in and then quietly said, "Don't wreck it. You can get away with cutting holes in crates, but if you wreck the machine you could go to jail. It's a valuable piece of equipment."

"I could cut the rubber pipes that feed the air to the motors. Or I could stuff the exhaust. Someone once stuffed the exhaust of a car that I had. The car would start but it died right away. I don't think that I can wreck it, it's built like a tank, I would need explosives. The hull is solid steel," And hitting the hull with his hammer he said, "My hammer doesn't even put a dent in it."

"I would leave it be. In some ways, it's good that the airport is using nonlethal ways to discourage geese."

"I can't bear to have the airport succeed with anything. I grew up around here and I saw what a mess they made of Jamaica Bay."

"You don't have to express your feelings by wrecking things. You can express yourself in other ways."

"I can't wreck it. I might be able to cut a hydraulic hose if I had a sharper pocket knife"

"They will notice the cut hose and replace it."

"I could try to re-route some of the hoses. Uncouple a few of them and put them back in the wrong places. Switch the boom hydraulics with the steering. Switch the drive to the paddle wheels with the boom. You know, switch the hoses around. They won't be able to operate the floating combined harvester if the controls don't work."

"You don't have a wrench to undo the nuts that secure the hoses! You don't have a monkey wrench! Before today, you had never heard of Edward Abbey!" Tanisha said.

Marty took off two layers of clothes and then his shirt. Then he put the two outer layers back on. Taking the shirt, he balled it up and stuffed it up the machine's exhaust pipe before declaring, "I'm going back to my first idea. I've stuffed the exhaust. At least I've done something."

Marty would have liked to have seen the airport disappear, but he was getting satisfaction from saving geese. He took a Budweiser from his top pocket, snapped the pull tab, and gulped it.

"Do you have a Bud for me?" Tanisha asked.

"I have another can of Bud on the boat. Let's retrace our steps back to the boat and get out of here," Marty replied.

Grunge

The trip back to the marina took a while, as Marty slowly motored against the current. There was no moon, but the lights from the shore lit the surface of the water. Buoys 9 and 10 were lit red and green and were easy to find. Marty steered a compass course of 47 degrees from the buoys until he saw the shadow of the marina breakwater. He then made a sharp right and followed the line of the breakwater pilings. It was three A.M.

Inside the breakwater the water was still, broken only by the ripples that small shiny fish made on the surface. The boat's motion was steady now and there was no longer a swell. A helicopter passing above broke the silence. Tanisha motioned for Marty to kill the boat's navigation lights, but Marty objected saying, "He's not looking for us. It's a police helicopter. They often land at Floyd Bennett Field, if we suddenly kill the lights it will only make them suspicious."

Marty located his dock from memory. He located his slip by counting off the slips from the end of the dock. His was the fifth and he docked with a skill that he had learned over time.

"There is something greasy on my arm," Tanisha said as the boat stopped and she felt around.

"I greased the winch. Wipe it off on this rag," Marty replied, and he went off to secure a second line on the bow.

"Can you do that later? I need to get on land," Tanisha said.

"Hold my hand as you step off," said Marty, as he finished tying the line.

Tanisha stepped off but she stumbled as she came ashore, "It feels like the ground is moving. It still feels like I'm traveling over waves. I'm going up and down and I'm off the boat."

"Hold onto me; you will feel okay soon," Marty replied, knowing that sometimes motion sickness lasted for days.

They walked silently to the end of the dock, past the benches, the store with the icebox, and the vending machines "The ground's not moving, do you see the light in the guards' hut? Is there a guard?" Tanisha asked.

"No, they leave the light on. Nobody will be here until the morning. I once painted my boat at night and nobody saw me," Marty replied.

"Why did you do that?"

"The marina charges 11 dollars a foot to paint boat bottoms. I saved a lot of money by doing it myself at night."

"Wouldn't you be able to see the paint better in daylight?"

"They don't allow you to paint your own boat. The only way you can do it is to sneak in at night."

"Why?"

"It's one way that they have to make money. I did it in May the year before last."

"When can we leave?"

"We will have to wait here until dawn. We'll be noticed if we get on the bus at this hour. The marina store will also open in the morning. We should leave when it gets light but before the store opens. I don't want to be seen."

"Let's go back to your boat and sleep until it gets light," Tanisha said.

Marty nodded okay.

On the trip back, Marty watched the distant lights of the Rockaways. A row of lights lit most of the dock, but there were unlit areas between the circles of light. In the dark, Marty found himself stepping on shellfish shells and crab-leg shells that crunched in the silence. Looking back towards the marina, all he saw was darkness. Looking up, he noticed that there was too much light pollution to see stars. The water reflected what light there was.

The air was still cool and smelled of seaweed and shellfish, and Marty liked this. Tanisha was walking more confidently now and stopped hanging on to him.

Back at his boat, Marty saw just how small it was compared to the boats next to it. He had to climb down to his boat from the dock while the other boat owners had to climb up. His boat rocked dangerously as he stepped on board, but it righted itself as he moved to the center. He unlocked the cabin door, switched on the light in the cabin, and climbed in. There was only one place to sleep, at the front on some blue cushions. There was just room for two people in the V berth, and the mast support separated the berths. Tanisha didn't ask Marty where she should sleep, she just pulled up the hood on her anorak and curled up in the berth to the right of the mast support. Marty went back outside to look around before returning to the cabin; he took the berth to the left of the support.

Tanisha yawned before saying, "The boat is not rocking anymore. I like the sound of water lapping against the side, it's relaxing. I don't feel nausea anymore.

"We are inside the breakwater. The breakwater kills the waves."

"It's cold. Do you have a blanket?"

"Yes," he said, passing her a blanket.

"I'm still nervous and excited, I'm sleepy but I can't sleep."

"Try counting sheep, or geese."

"Funny guy."

"If there had been geese at the airport, what would you have done?"

"I did wreck the cages. I could also have tried to lead the geese away from the airport by laying a trail of corn."

"The airport is surrounded by water. There isn't a route out," replied Marty.

"I noticed," said Tanisha.

"Golf courses hire specially trained dogs to chase away geese."

"That's cruel."

"Seriously, did you come up with a plan to rescue the geese?"

"When will the geese gather by the airport?"

"Just before they molt, in about a month. They like the calm sheltered waters by the airport."

"We have time. If we think about it, we can figure it out."

"Before the department of agriculture, the USDA, rounds up the geese and gasses them?"

"Yes, we'll figure it out."

"They claim that gassing the geese is painless, but when they are gassed they have convulsions and struggle to breathe and try to fly." There was a long, long silence, "What do you think will happen with the animal crates that you wrecked?"

"I thought that you were asleep."

"Maybe the USDA will replace the crates. Maybe they won't. Maybe they won't notice the holes that I cut and still try to crate the geese. I have no idea what will happen if they do this. The geese might stay put in the crate or form an orderly line and walk out, or they might stampede," Marty replied.

At five A.M., Tanisha woke Marty, "I'm fully awake now. I'm cold and your blanket isn't helping much. I'm going to walk down to the shower in the marina bathroom, a warm shower will take away the chill. Then we should go to the main road and look for a bus."

As they walked back down the dock, the eastern sky began to lighten. In broad daylight, one would see seagull droppings, random shellfish shells, and loose screws. But at dawn, there was also a layer of moisture, as the night's dew made the dock slippery.

Tanisha gripped Marty as she walked unsteadily to the shower, which was in a woodshed by the car park at the end of the dock. It was a single shower with a small bench for sitting, but there were no towels or soap. There was a light in the shower, but no lampshade, and Marty noticed that there was no lock. The shower contributed to the feeling of grunge.

"Can you stand guard outside? There isn't a lock," Tanisha asked.

"Sure," Marty replied.

He stood quietly by the broken door until his curiosity got to him, and he turned to look inside. Staring, he saw the outline of Tanisha, and he almost ran when he saw her white eyes staring back at him. Marty, embarrassed, quickly turned away and made a mental note that what he had done was wrong.

Some ten minutes later, Tanisha emerged from the shower, having changed from her black pants and top to her usual bright colors, "Did you look when I was in the shower?" she asked.

"Sorry," Marty replied. And Tanisha laughed before asking, "Our eyes met. I knew that you were looking at me. Are you going to take a shower?"

"I might not bathe today. It feels good to take a bath after not bathing for a bit. I once held off for a week and the bath felt great," Marty replied.

"Don't you get zits?"

"I get zits and pimples and I pop them. If I haven't had a blackhead for a few weeks I start to miss them. I guess it's a lower-class thing."

"That's gross."

Tanisha then started to head towards the road, but Marty caught her arm and stopped her, saying, "We will be noticed if we get on the bus at this hour."

"Why did you cut the holes in the crates? If you hadn't wrecked them, we could have gone home," Tanisha said.

"I used to always think things out before I acted, but I got headaches and never did anything. There were always two sides to everything. Now, I try to go with my first impulse."

"You are too old to act crazy."

"We have to wait until it's light before we catch the bus."

"I'm going to sit by the shed at the end of the dock and watch the sun come up."

"Do young people still do that?"

"I do."

Tanisha sat in semidarkness for 15 minutes before she said, "Watch the sky. The sun is starting to come out in the east. Look at the colors from the first rays. I see yellow, orange, and red. Soon you will be able to feel the sun's rays on your face."

By six A.M., the sun had risen and it was getting warmer. The dock was drying and land birds began to appear. The whine of car tires on Flatbush Avenue and the constant chirping of crickets broke the silence. The warm breeze carried the smell of new-mown grass, replacing the low-tide smell of the bay.

Leaving the marina and crossing the avenue, Marty slowed and held Tanisha's arm. "We need to lie low for a few days," he said.

"Nobody saw us," Tanisha replied.

But seeing the bus coming, and feeling some relief after they had not been stopped, Marty said, "The security guard at the airport might have, he might have seen us."

Tanisha didn't reply, but before they got on the bus she said, "You are a sly one."

"What?" Marty asked.

"You are not so wholesome. You are a 73-year-old voyeur who wrecks stuff and then looks out for the cops," Tanisha said.

PART TWO

32.   DEAD HORSE BAY

32.   DEAD HORSE BAY

The Duck Commander

"If it sounds like a duck ... "
—*Phil Robertson,* Happy, Happy, Happy: My Life and Legacy as the Duck
Commander

Marty had a scheme to move the geese away from the airport away
using a duck call. He figured that his boat was small enough to hide and
that he'd head out to the marshes south of JFK, hide his boat, and practice calling ducks and geese away from the airport.

With his Social Security check, Marty bought a Duck Commander,
and on Tuesday it arrived in the mail. The Duck Commander was a five-
inch long reed instrument that made a sound like a duck. Duck hunters
used them to attract ducks, and then they shot them. Marty planned to
use the call to lure the ducks away from the airport and out of harm's
way. He'd ordered the "Camo Max" model, which had a double reed and
army camouflage paint. The Duck Commander had the company's logo
on the package, showing a mallard drake with wings cupped and legs
lowered, looking down to land, and then presumably to be shot.

He first practiced blowing into the duck call in his living room, and
then when it got too loud he moved out in the street. At first, he couldn't
get a noise from the call, but eventually he found a combination of hand
position and air pressure, and he could make the basic sound of a duck.
He learned to make a clean, crisp, "quack."

It was a solid plan. If it worked with ducks, he could, with a lower-
pitched note, also call geese, and with practice he might also be able to
call mute swans and snowy owls, all of which were likely to be shot or

gassed if they stayed near Kennedy. He wasn't doing anything illegal. It wasn't duck hunting season. He wasn't hunting ducks.

Out on Jamaica Bay, from the marsh just south of Kennedy airport, Marty had a view of the airport with New York City in the background. It was a great view, and Marty could make out most of the tall buildings in Manhattan in the distance. In the middle ground, white smoke rose from the chimneys of the Ravenswood Power Generating Station; otherwise the sky was clear. Close up, there were the sunlit greens of Jamaica Bay's salt-marsh islands. Marty could see that there were waterfowl on the strip of land near the airport, but he could not make out whether they were ducks or geese.

Marty floated his lone duck decoy out towards the airport and stood watching it with his back to the wind. The sun was still in the east. It reflected on his left and would hide him a little from any approaching ducks. He'd figured that the ducks would land into the wind, and the first call he made was "WI-CH, WI-CH, WI-CH, WI-CH, WI-CH," which he made softly, like "quack, quack, quack, quack, and quack." The open space muffled the call, so he cupped his hands to direct the sound before he called again. The wide-open space still swallowed up the sound, leaving Marty to feel small and insignificant.

"WI-CH, WI-CH, WI-CH, WI-CH, WI-CH"

Two mallards, a male and a female, came in from behind him. They turned into the wind, cupped their wings, and lowered their legs as they came into land, just like the duck on the Duck Commander logo. Although these mallards were not from the airport, Marty was attracting ducks.

The ducks leveled out before finally cupping their wings again and splashing down. The second duck almost collided with Marty's duck decoy, which did not move over.

Marty called again, "WI-CH, WI-CH, WI-CH, WI-CH, WI-CH," and the two ducks that had arrived moved their heads. To Marty, the ducks seemed restless and unlikely to stay. They dipped their heads and then swam about two feet before they dipped their heads again, like they were trying to find something in the water. Marty figured that they were looking for food, and he had brought just the thing: homemade spinach-and-corn pudding. He had made the pudding from spinach and corn on an egg base, and it floated with the help of a block of Styrofoam. Marty floated the pudding on the block of Styrofoam, pushed it out towards the ducks, and when they were close enough the ducks started to peck at it.

With one problem solved, Marty changed his hand placement on the Duck Commander to get a lower note than before. He called "WHAT, WHAT, WHAT, WHAT, WHAT," the greeting call of Canada geese. No matter that the nearby geese were possibly resident New York City geese. They were originally from Canada.

"WHAT, WHAT, WHAT, WHAT, WHAT"

"what, what, what, what, what" He started loud and got softer.

Five large Canada geese flying in V formation turned to check out what was going on, and Marty continued to call until they landed about 50 yards out. There was a loud splash as the 20-pound birds with six-foot wingspans dropped into the water. Marty tried to bring them in closer, calling "CLUCK, CLUCK, CLUCK, CLUCK, CLUCK." He was feeling elated from his new-found ability to call geese and mimic their feeding sounds with "CLUCK, CLUCK, CLUCK." He opened a can of beer and pushed out another spinach-and-corn pudding, as by now the first pudding was gone and the birds were trying to eat the string that held his duck decoy in place.

The geese went for the second pudding and began to make soft feeding chatter: "tick-it, tick-it, tick-it, tick-it, tick-it," which Marty copied and amplified on the Duck Commander. He hit gold with this sound and soon attracted five more geese, two duck couples, and a lonesome duck hen. It was time to call more geese.

After two more calls, Marty had almost finished his beer. He had come to giving away his position by talking to the birds. Two birds taking off interrupted his "You'll be safe here, away from the airport" speech. He shut up quickly and returned to his thoughts.

Calling birds was different from spiking trees, freeing caged animals, or sabotaging equipment and other stuff that had sent some eco-warriors to jail. Calling birds without shooting them was legal. Maybe, given time, he could call all the birds from the airport, but where would the birds go from here? The two birds that had just left the marsh were on their way back to the airport, and once he ran out of corn-and-spinach pudding the other birds would likely follow.

Spurred by Tanisha's recommendation, Marty had started to read *The Monkey Wrench Gang* by Edward Abbey. He even took a special liking for one of the characters, George Washington Hayduke. He copied Hayduke by throwing his empty beer can into the water and opening another one. Bird calling required serious thought.

Bottle Beach

After their trip out to Kennedy, Marty and Tanisha decided to meet up on the Dead Horse Bay beach to discuss future tactics. This was Bottle Beach, Marty remembered as he felt a bottle underfoot as he walked along. They had taken different routes to get to the beach: Marty took the trail from Flatbush Avenue through the trees and the reeds inland from the beach, while Tanisha took the easier route, walking along the beach from the marina.

Marty was in a good mood when he arrived five minutes early. He'd heard a yellow warbler sing "sweet, sweet, sweet, little-more-sweet" on the trail down from Flatbush Avenue. It was enough, his favorite bird, but he also would have enjoyed seeing the small, egg-yolk-yellow bird in the trees. He took off his coat as he walked up to the wrecked cabin cruiser that lay on the beach. He sat on the half-buried boat as he waited for Tanisha to arrive.

When he saw her walking towards him, he noticed that she was wearing a purple tank top, blue shorts, and dark sunglasses. The sunglasses reflected the sun and moved with it as she walked over the beach.

A storm had swept the cabin cruiser from its mooring in Sheepshead Bay to where they were meeting. It washed up on the beach and was now abandoned there, laying on the beach with half its hull buried in the sand. Like any place where there was a wreck, this part of the beach had a feeling of sadness. Marty had chosen this spot because he knew that nobody would be around to listen in on the conversation.

Marty got up as Tanisha approached and Tanisha smiled a greeting. She then put down a glass bottle that she was carrying, kicked off her shoes, picked up a sea shell, and began to run her toes through the wet sand.

"What's in the bottle?" Marty asked.

"I picked it up on the beach. It's a pretty bottle. I was going to empty it and take it home, but there is stuff living in it," Tanisha replied. She then held the bottle up to the light and said, "There is a little sand crab on the bottom." And handing the bottle to Marty said, "Can you see it?"

Marty stared into the bottle. "I see it. It's almost clear and looks to be the same color as the sand. There is also a brown beetle. There is life in the bottle," he replied.

Marty handed it back and Tanisha put it down on the beach.

"Are you okay taking charge of the goose rescue?" she asked.

"Just because I'm in charge of my boat does not mean that I want to take charge of the goose rescue," replied Marty.

"But ..." Tanisha muttered.

"It's straightforward. I'm captain of my boat, and you are in charge of the goose rescue," said Marty.

"But you are not emotionally involved with the geese. You will be better at it than me."

"This is an opportunity for you. You could be the first black eco-warrior."

"Like the first black President?"

"Yes, like Obama."

"You do know that there were six black presidents before Obama?"

"The ones before Obama were only a little bit black."

"If they were one-sixteenth black, they would have been counted as black in the census."

"Obama got the Nobel Prize," said Marty.

"There is no point being the first black eco-warrior. Nobody is going to get the Nobel Prize for rescuing geese," replied Tanisha.

Marty laughed, and then they both fell silent as a dog walker went by.

"So, what do you know about geese?" asked Tanisha.

"I've watched them flying overhead in winter. I noticed that they often take the same flight path. Why are they rounding up geese?" replied Marty.

"It's complicated, the local geese had nothing to do with the downing of US Airways Flight 1549. The geese that Sully hit were migratory birds flying at 13,000 feet. They might have been flying for days, climbing steadily. Taking advantage of air currents and eddies. They like the cold air up there. They flew in from Canada.

"The roundup of local geese is a panic reaction. It won't make airplane travel any safer. It's a bit like the roundup of Japanese in California after the Japanese attacked Pearl Harbor. And like the roundup of Japanese in California, it's wrong.

"It's public relations. The airlines spend a lot of money getting people to fly," replied Tanisha.

Tanisha dropped her serious look, took off her sunglasses, climbed into the boat, moved to the front, and dangled her feet over the side, close to where Marty was standing.

"Come sit with me. I can't think on my feet," she said.

Marty pulled himself up onto the wreck. "Why do the geese choose to molt by Kennedy?"

"They can't fly when they are replacing their flight feathers. They stay by the water so that they can escape from predators. At molt time, they like calm, inland waters. The water by Kennedy is ideal."

"So, who is rounding up the geese at Kennedy?" Marty asked.

"Again, it's complicated. The Port Authority runs the airport, and they want to get rid of the geese. They want to get rid of all geese within a seven-mile radius of LaGuardia and JFK airports.

"They contract with the United States Department of Agriculture Wildlife Service, the USDA, who act like hired assassins," replied Tanisha.

"And?" Marty asked.

"The USDA has to get permission before they can kill the geese."

"From who?"

"From the Park Service and the Mayor."

"Anyone else?"

"From the feds, the National Park Service, the Department of the Interior."

"And they all say go ahead?" Marty asked.

"It's likely," replied Tanisha.

"Do we have any friends?" Marty asked.

"Not really, but the Park Service does not want to be seen to be involved," replied Tanisha.

"This is a nightmare. We don't even know when the geese are to be rounded up."

"It's usually in July, when they're molting. They're easy to catch when they can't fly. My husband works security at Kennedy, and he will let me know the date."

"Can you get anyone else from Goose Watch to help?"

"Don will, he has been out to the airport, and he's willing to go back."

"Who's Don?"

"He was a duck hunter, but he's changed sides. He says that he shot a lot more ducks than he ate. You will either love him or hate him. He tends to be divisive."

"We are going to have to interfere with the roundup," said Marty.

"How?" asked Tanisha.

"We are going to have to work that out."

They left together, taking the direct route home along the beach and up the makeshift path to the marina. Before leaving the beach, Tanisha poured out the water, the crab, the beetle, the seaweed, and the sand from the bottle. She rinsed it before packing it to take it home. It was a clear bottle with a raised pattern at the top and bottom and an ornate neck. The label on it read: "Old-Fashioned Tasty Creamy Root Beer—You'll Love It."

Potato Wedges in Duck Fat

"Better a cruel truth than a comfortable delusion"
—Edward Abbey: A Voice Crying in the Wilderness, Notes from a Secret Journal

After his success calling ducks, Marty decided to look for a helper so that he could call geese. He planned to move the geese twice by calling them twice; he planned to move the geese far away from the airport. His last attempt to call ducks had been a success and if he could, with a double hop, move the geese further away from the airport, he thought that they would have little chance of finding their way back.

The search for a helper took a while until Marty remembered that Tanisha knew a guy, Don, who used to hunt ducks in the Chesapeake Bay. Don might know goose calls, and if he was as reformed as Tanisha said he was, he would be willing to help.

Wednesday morning came and Don turned up looking the part. Marty studied his appearance. Don looked like a character from *Duck Dynasty*. He wore an American flag bandana, baggy camouflage jean bib overalls with suspenders, and he had long black hair and a black beard that had a few white streaks.

Marty lost a coin toss with Don and so had to steer Soft Kitty over to the airport. Marty sat to starboard, facing Don as he motored out towards a small unnamed island at Broad Creek Marsh. The island was about a thousand yards south of the airport. The boat tilted because Don was well built. He was shorter than Marty but more than made up for this with a combination of muscle and fat, so his side of the boat pitched toward the water.

"Is the boat safe?" Don asked.

"Yes, it's just unevenly loaded," Marty replied.

"Together we weigh over 300 pounds," Don said.

"Don't move about too much," Marty said.

"There's nowhere to move."

"Sit still, but try to keep your weight in the center of the boat."

Don sat very still and Marty decided that this would be a good time to ask him about the long bag that he carried. Marty asked, "Do you still hunt geese?"

"No."

"What's in your bags?"

"This one has my single shot, break-action shotgun and this one has my lunch."

"How much ammunition do you have?"

"I have four three-inch magnum shells, but it's old ammunition and it might not work."

"You're not planning to shoot something, are you?"

"Oh no, the gun is for protection. I was once attacked by a pair of geese. They hissed as they charged at me. They broke my skin with their beaks and they beat me with their wings. I might have been near their nest."

"Did you try to shoot the geese?"

"I missed!"

"Why didn't you shoot again when they charged?"

"I had to reload, it's single-shot."

"Don't shoot anything today."

Just then, Marty had an epiphany: Geese were not always helpless and docile. If their goslings were in danger, they would fight back.

Some 30 minutes later, Marty recognized the unnamed small island covered with marsh grass that he had visited on his last trip out, and he started to look for the beer can he had thrown into the water. He wanted to be sure of his location. Seeing the can, half-submerged, Marty was sure that he had found the spot. Marty cut the motor and threw out the anchor into four feet of water.

"Are we going to call the geese from the boat or from the island?" Don asked.

"We can stay on board," Marty replied.

Don pushed the duck decoy into the water.

"Hold on," Said Marty.

"Why?" Don asked.

"You have to create a scene that is attractive to geese. Put the decoy on a string and throw it out into the current by the cattail, the tide is coming in for the next two hours. Then you have to talk to the birds. It's not just sounds. Orchestrate the calls. Tell the birds a story. The decoy lets them know that it's safe here. Your job is to tell them that there is food and that it's a fun place. Punctuate your calls with happy sounds," Marty replied.

Don stood with his back to the sun, "You've not done this before today," he said, and immediately he put his Honky Tonk goose call into his mouth and he began to call geese until he had called 20 or so.

Marty floated a spinach-and-corn pudding on a Styrofoam block for the geese and, as he was feeling hungry, he started to eat one himself.

"Aren't those for the geese?" Don asked.

"I'm only eating one," Marty said. He handed Don a pudding, "Don't eat the Styrofoam."

Don gagged, "I brought my own lunch."

"What have you got?"

"A ham sandwich and some potato wedges in duck fat. My wife watches Chef John on YouTube, and when I told her that I was going to help you call geese she went to the supermarket and bought some duck fat."

Marty finished his spinach-and-corn pudding and opened a beer, "It's time to move on. Pull the string to bring the decoy in. They won't miss the one duck," said Marty.

Marty then pulled in the anchor and motioned for Don to join him at the back of the boat. Clearing the marsh grass, Marty headed south; about another thousand yards into the bay there was a tiny island that he had seen on the way in. If Marty remembered correctly, this island was Winhole Hassock. It was Don's turn to steer, and with Don at the port side of the boat, the port side was down.

Winhole Hassock offered a little cover with bushes and scrub inland, but it was still mostly covered with marsh grass, that barely rose above high-tide. The island was flat, maybe a hundred yards long, with several small freshwater pools; the only place for them to hide was among the grasses. Don beached the boat on the side opposite the airport, and they both stepped off the boat onto the low-lying land

When they got there, Don's first question was, "Why do we have to call the birds twice?"

"It's a system that I thought up to move the birds away from the airport, step by step," Marty replied.

"Why can't you move them long-distance?" asked Don.

"They can't hear long-distance. If you just called geese from here, you would get the wrong geese," Marty replied.

"Can you make the calls this time?"

"Just get on with it. I'll take over when you're tired."

"Where can we hide?"

"Lie on your stomach in the grass and pull your cap over your head. Nobody will see you behind your beard."

"Where are you going?"

"I'll lie with you."

Marty then took out a notebook and, as the geese arrived, tried to figure out where they were coming from. He put checks in columns marked "airport geese" and "other geese." Mostly, though, he couldn't tell by watching them arrive where they came from. Marty started to look around, but they did not fly in straight lines. They came in slow curves in a V formation, and to confuse recognition even more, they would often change the shape of the V as they flew in family combinations. They would also often pass overhead before turning back to land, making it even harder to make out where they were from.

Frustrated, Marty got up and walked to the nearest pool, where he looked down and put his hand in the water to check its temperature. Geese like a comfortable temperature. It was warmer than last month, and looking into the water Marty could see the heads and the almost-translucent tails of tadpoles. There were also two newts, which Marty thought were ugly because of the dark spots that they had on their backs. The marsh was coming alive. On the surface of the water there were mosquitoes, pond skaters, and some dragonfly eggs were floating by on fallen leaves.

Don interrupted Marty's idling to come over and say, "I'm tired, you have a go," handing the goose call to Marty.

The goose call was about six inches long and had two sections. Marty proceeded to pull it apart. He removed the reed from the soundboard and noticed the notch that held it in place. It was different from his Duck Commander. The Honky Tonk had a single reed while the Duck Commander had a double, it also had a wider bore, but when you blew into them, each sounded like a kazoo.

Marty then put the Honky Tonk back together and he examined its cosmetics: the picture of the flying goose on its sleeve and the logo that read, "Final approach, speak the language." He then blew into the narrow end, but nothing came out; all he could hear was the air rushing through. Don interrupted him, saying, "Turn the call around."

Blowing into the fat end of the call, the noise was pretty loud. Marty then began to hum into the call in the same way he had with his Duck Commander, and he got the sound that he was looking for. The sound was deeper and louder than the duck call, and producing the sound required more effort. He began to understand why Don was tired, but not wanting to let on about this, he moved back to the grass, laid down low, and started to call geese.

A few minutes later Marty took a breather. That's when Don handed him a lanyard for the goose call, saying, "Clip it on, hang the call around your neck. Try to look the part."

Marty hesitated before putting the lanyard around his neck, as he was not sure that he wanted to look like a duck hunter. Don resolved Marty's hesitancy by taking the lanyard, opening it, and put it over Marty's head.

"You still don't look right. You don't have a beard. Let me blacken your face. Your white head sticks out among the scrub. I'm going to make you look like a duck hunter," Don said.

Don then took out a piece of cork, lit his cigarette lighter, and set the cork alight. He let the cork burn for a while before he killed the flame. After the cork cooled, he smiled as he rubbed the charcoal-like dust from the cork onto Marty's face

Marty protested, but not strong enough to stop Don from also smearing the cork ash onto his ears.

"Do you ever lotion? Your skin feels like sandpaper," Don asked.

"Let me be," Marty said.

"You can do this. If only you get into the part," Don replied.

Marty watched two geese land into the wind. They sort of splashed down after braking. One almost collided with Marty's duck decoy after it failed to make room for the incoming goose. The landing geese cupped their wings to slow down and then lowered their feet to break their fall. They still went underwater, but quickly scrambled back to the surface. He watched two more land. They repeated the steps, and it wasn't too long before there were several dozen geese in the water in front of them.

"Let's sneak away and leave the geese here," Marty said.

"How?" Don asked.

"Push yourself up on your elbows and crawl slowly back away from them."

"They won't stay."

"They won't see us go. We'll leave them here"

"Where is the boat?"

"It's behind you."

"Let's turn around now, my elbows are hurting, it will be easier to crawl forward."

"Just a bit further; we are almost there. This was a really successful trip."

"Successful?"

"You just don't want me to succeed."

"I'm not sure that you did. If you don't shoot the geese that you have called, they will eventually fly off in all directions."

"That's good. If they fly off in all directions from here then only a few will return to the airport. We're further away, do the math, and from out here the view of the airport is only a small arc. The airport made a big arc from the first island."

The Squall

"Wind before rain, the sun will shine again." Traditional sailing adage: If the wind freshens before rain arrives, a squall will generally be short-lived and conditions will probably revert to what they were before the squall.

The return trip from the marsh just south of Kennedy airport to Dead Horse Bay started well. Soft Kitty was moving nicely. Marty had both sails up; there were clear skies and a southwest wind.

Marty's mood broke when Don, who was sitting next to him in the cockpit, said, "I really feel bad about the time when I hunted ducks."

"Does Tanisha know?" asked Marty.

"I'm telling you," Don replied.

"Why?" asked Marty.

"I killed a lot more ducks than I ate. I didn't even retrieve some of the ducks that I shot. One day I shot at everything that moved," Don's gaze was directed downward.

"You are going to make amends, by saving geese."

"You don't have a plan to rescue the geese."

"I'll come up with something," said Marty giving Don a reassuring smile.

"Will I get to help?"

"Yes."

"Thanks."

"Did you ever use a toller?" Marty asked.

"What's that," asked Don.

"A live decoy, honking to call in other geese. Like a church bell calls people to church," Marty replied.

"I've never heard of tollers"

"It's illegal now, but there are still hunters that use them. I'm fascinated by the fact that all of our domestic geese are descendants of freed tollers."

"Yes …" said Don, as he again looked down.

"Don't look so sad."

"… I already feel bad about hunting."

"Sorry," Marty replied. And they both fell silent.

Passing under the Gil Hodges Memorial Marine Park Bridge, Marty was happy to be almost home. To his left was the beach with a row of houses and trees behind it. Ahead, he could make out the lighthouse at Breezy Point, and to his right, he could make out the Parachute Jump, the Wonder Wheel, the Thunderbolt, and the Coney Island Cyclone at the Coney Island Amusement Park.

He was close to the Rockaways in 30 feet of water, maybe a hundred yards offshore, and inland from buoy 20 when the sky to the west started to darken. The sky was gray with a line of black clouds heading his way. There was a flash of lightning, followed by two or three more, followed by thunder as the sky erupted. A squall was a mile away and moving toward them.

Looking at the approaching storm, Don said, "It's going to rain. Can I go inside?"

Marty didn't reply, and Don ducked inside the cabin.

Marty expected that having a sail up when strong winds hit would capsize the boat. He had to turn the boat into the wind and drop the sails before the squall arrived. But after the turn into the wind, he was heading towards the beach. If he didn't drop the sails quickly, he would run aground. There was no option except to work fast. He furled the jib. Then he secured the tiller to maintain his course and went forward to the mast and released the mainsail. He tied it to the boom with the sail ties that he had been holding in his teeth. Returning to the helm, he felt a stillness before the squall hit, before the boat leaned over at a crazy angle, before he felt fear—a fear that lasted until the boat sprung back into an upright position. It was then that the hail fell. Half-inch balls of ice bounced on the deck and rolled across the cockpit. They stung his face and his bare legs. Don, probably alerted by the hammering of the hail, appeared at the cabin door and started to laugh. Don got a kick out of seeing Marty being pelted by hail.

With the sails down, Marty turned the boat away from the beach. The boat slowed, but he had little control, and the boat was moving downwind. Using more force than necessary, he started the outboard engine by pulling hard on the starter cord, and since the hail had all but blinded him, he steered in small circles, making a violent turn each time he crossed through the wind.

Luckily, the boat was not in the shipping channel. It was still in deep water. If the boat would stay pretty much where it was, and if it's bouncing about didn't throw him or Don off, they would be all right.

Eventually, the wind died down, the hail stopped, and Marty saw another small boat close by. Don again appeared in the cabin door and again started to laugh. The other guy's boat was much smaller than Marty's, a small skiff named Pretzel. It had a single seat that the skipper was struggling to remain on while his boat bounced on the waves.

The guy on the other boat shouted, "Hello!" and then waved.

Marty waved back.

Marty didn't start to laugh straight away, but the guy waved again. Don was still laughing, and this got to him. Marty and Don were both laughing, and Marty was still soaked when the sun came out.

The boat was a mess. A pot had fallen off the sink and broke. A box of tea had spilled. Everything had fallen off the boat's shelf.

Although the weather was now fine, Marty did not put the sails back up for the rest of the trip home. He was not looking for another sailing adventure, so he slowly motored over the long waves, the ocean's swell. At one point, the water looked like it was not level. It looked like the boat was going up a curve to the top of a hill. They could see Coney Island and Brooklyn in the distance on top of the hill.

Entering the channel into Dead Horse Bay, Marty slowed the engine and looked questioningly at Don.

Don looked pissed but didn't say anything.

Marty asked, "What?"

"After you got the sails down you had no control of the boat," replied Don.

"I started the engine."

"Weren't you afraid?"

"I was too busy. I would have appreciated help."

"The boat almost tipped over. We could have been thrown overboard."

"I could have been. You were inside."

"I don't like sailboats. I won't be sailing with you again."

Marty was concerned, as Don had not helped with the boat during the squall. But also puzzled because Don had not looked scared when the squall hit. Don seemed more worried about the past, about his days as a hunter, about the days when he had killed too many ducks.

The Dead Zone

"A portion of Jamaica Bay that borders the airport includes a 'dead' section called Grassy Bay along the edge of runway 13R/31L (Bay Runway) that was dredged to 60 feet to construct JFK in the 1950s."
—Jamaica Bay and Kennedy Airport: A Multidisciplinary Environmental Study

Marty was starting to have feelings for geese, but he had strong feelings for the places where he had played as a kid and which airport construction had ruined. One such place was the so-called dead zone; he'd visited it recently with Tanisha when they went to look for geese at the airport. The trip out there had reminded him of the place, and now he wanted to go back to the dead zone and look for any signs of plant or aquatic life. On a previous trip out, he had noticed that there was no life on the water surface, but maybe there was life if you looked down. He had brought with him a home made hydroscope and he was going to use the hydroscope to look underneath the water.

The day Marty chose to visit the dead zone was windy, and it looked as though it might rain. He was alone. Tanisha said that the trip had nothing to do with geese but was the result of his lifelong dislike of the airport. Marty normally liked his own company, but today he was a little scared. There were few boats out on the water, and he shivered as he realized that if he got into trouble there would be nobody around to help.

It was too windy to sail. He was going to motor all the way. Sometimes he trailed a "last chance rope" rope behind the boat so that if he fell overboard, he could grab it, but with the rough water he could not get the rope to float away from the boat's propeller. The engine would stall if the rope snagged in the propeller, so he brought the rope in. He tied the engine shut-off to his wrist. Now, if he went overboard the engine would cut out. Still, he knew that getting back on board would not be easy. He wasn't as agile as he had been when he was younger.

Breezy Point was that and more, and Marty had difficulty controlling the boat. There was a two-foot chop that pounded his small boat and covered his face with spray. He would check the water after the bridge, and if it was still rough, he could turn back and head home.

Ducking under the shelter of the Gil Hodges Memorial Marine Park Bridge, Marty checked the weather forecast on 1010 WINS. There was a three-car pileup on the Major Deegan Expressway. There were traffic jams on most of the bridges and tunnels, and there was a tractor-trailer overturned on the NJ Turnpike. Rod Stewart followed the news. He was singing "Old Man River." The song's native strength made Stewart's effort sound weak, so Marty switched the radio off. He then tried his marine radio, but the battery was dead, so he went back to what he always did; he looked at the sky. There was a storm brewing over Staten Island, but it looked like it wasn't coming his way. Inland of the Gil Hodges bridge the water was calmer, Marty was grateful for this and continued towards the second bridge.

On this stretch, he was in the shelter of land, and he tried to think ahead. After the second bridge there was East Broad Channel and then the small islands Winhole Hassack, Hissock Manor, Yellow Bar Hassock, the Raunt, and Jack's Hole. These islands stuck out of the marsh and rose only a few feet above it; grasses such as bluestem, switchgrass, and seaside goldenrod crowded the islands. Some of them were difficult to identify, as they apparently merged into one another, but this didn't matter if he was able to stay in the channel that wound its way around them.

Feeling warmer, Marty removed his waterproof jacket and dried his wet face. He could see the large hangar at Kennedy from half a mile out and knew that he was in the right place. To get closer, all he had to do was thread his way through the shallow East Broad Channel until he got to Grassy Bay and the dead zone. When he got to the dead zone, the water depth would plunge to 50 feet and the water's color would change from blue to gray and black. It smelled like rotten eggs, and when you looked down you could no longer see what was beneath the surface. When the depth dropped off, Marty tied an extra length of rope to his anchor and tossed it overboard. He felt the rope go slack as it hit the bottom and hoped it would dig in.

Marty grew up east of Canarsie, where his parents owned a tobacco store. Jamaica Bay and the marshes had been his playground. He'd had a childhood friend, and in summer they spent most of their days near here in the rock pool by the breakwater. Looking inland, the area looked different now, it was more built-up. But the landmarks that he remembered had not changed, the church spire and the pier still stood out. What had changed was the water depth. When he was a kid the water here had been a few feet deep and you could stand on the bottom, now the water had been dredged to 50 feet and the excavated material had been used to form the land that became Kennedy Airport.

Feeling the anchor hold, he lowered the hydroscope into the water that wasn't blue and wasn't green. It was gray, but it was not entirely stagnant. There was a little movement downwards, with specs of black matter settling slowly like tapioca in bubble tea. Marty watched this until the noise of an engine and the wake from a speeding boat disturbed him. It was a police boat pulling up alongside him, and the two cops in the boat shouted, "Why are you out on a day like this? Are you looking for fish?"

"Looking for a wreck," Marty replied.

"What wreck?" the nearest cop asked.

"The steamer *Aretha* sank here in 1948," Marty replied.

"There is no wreck marked on our chart plotter," the nearest cop said.

"I don't have a chart plotter," Marty replied.

"This area is called the dead zone. There never was a wreck here," the second cop said.

"What?"

"I know how to spot a liar."

"I'm not doing anything wrong."

"You're obstructing navigation. What's that thing that you have in the water?"

"A hydroscope."

"It's obstructing navigation."

"It's not. Nobody comes here. There is a wreck."

"There isn't a wreck, I checked."

Marty started to get nervous but he stuck to his story, "It's not on the chart. I heard about it when I was a kid," he said.

"Can you show us what you have in the water?"

"It's going to be hard to pull up as it's weighted down with stones. It's a hydroscope; an upside-down periscope. You can see underwater with it."

"What's down there?"

"I saw something move. It looked like a mushroom."

"There is nothing alive down there. Can I see your Boating Safety Certificate?" the cop asked.

Marty remembered the safe boating course where he'd argued with the instructor and not gone back to take the test.

"I don't have it," Marty replied.

"It's mandatory," the second cop said.

"I don't have it."

The second cop handed Marty a citation. There was a 50 dollar fine for boating without a boating safety certificate.

"Let's go, Frank. He's just an old nut," the first cop said.

The second cop, Frank, said to Marty, "Don't you have anything better to do?"

Marty was not looking for a wreck. There was no wreck. The water was deep here. Wrecks happened where there were shallows. At the borrow pits the depth of the water dropped suddenly from 11 to 50 feet. Marty had watched the water depth drop as he approached and looked for signs of marine life. He thought about tying a flashlight to the end of the hydroscope, but he hadn't as he did not want to attract life into the area. But as it was, he could not see very far.

Marty had made the hydroscope himself. It was five feet long and four inches in diameter. He'd made it by cementing two straight white PVC pipes together. There was a 90-degree curved pipe set into the viewing end, with a small mirror cemented into the curve. The viewing end was open, but a piece of clear plastic sealed the end that went into the water. You looked into the curved end, and the 45-degree mirror reflected the view coming up from the bottom end. Thinking that he might improve on his design he had labelled the hydroscope the mark I.

Looking into the hydroscope, Marty could see only what was in the blue-and-green circle of light at the far end of the dark tube. He would have preferred to be able to look straight down the tube, as the scope's mirror distorted the view. It was black down there, like peering into a pit, into a mine, pitch dark. He needed more light at the end of the tube to illuminate the darkness. He needed a longer hydroscope, as there was nothing to see at the depth that this one could reach.

Marty was eight years old when the dredging began and created the scary 50-foot holes in the marsh that would become the dead zone. The holes were also known as borrow pits, depressions on the bay floor that crews mined for landfill material. The dredgers scooped up everything. A barge transported his childhood rock pool to the landfill that became New York's Kennedy airport. At age 11, Marty first started to notice the smells. The water in the deep holes was stagnant, as there was no oxygen to support aerobic life. He recognized the smell of stale eggs and garlic. The smell came from the sulfur and the phosphorus that was in the water. When Marty was 12, there was blackish clay on the bottom of the water where there once had been sand and rocks, and all the life in the water was gone.

Marty thought of Tanisha and her fight to save the geese. He wondered how long she had wanted this. It couldn't be more than a couple of years since US Airways Flight 1549 had landed in the Hudson River, and the roundups of geese had begun. His wish to see life come back to the dead zone had started 65 years ago, about 40 years before Tanisha was born.

The Mark II Hydroscope

Marty built the mark II hydroscope to look deeper into the water of the dead zone. He built it on the floor of his apartment where he had put down newspaper to make a makeshift workbench.

It took a day for Marty to build. It was like the mark I, except that Marty made it from larger pipes, and there was a flashlight duct-taped to the underwater end. The wider pipe, Marty thought, would give it a larger field of view and he added the flashlight in the hope that it would make seeing things in the murky water easier.

The mark II hydroscope was seven feet long and made from two three-foot-long, six-inch-diameter PVC pipe cemented together with solvent weld. It was two feet longer than the mark I. To keep the water out, Marty cemented a circle of Perspex to the end of the bottom drain pipe with waterproof glue. At the top, he cemented a 90-degree angled pipe, and at the point where the angle pipe curved, he cemented a vanity mirror at 45 degrees. That way, he could look horizontally into the scope and have the mirror reflect his view down.

At the upper end of the scope, Marty attached a hood to keep out the glare of the sun's light. And at the bottom of the pipe, he secured a coiled-rope hoop so that he could attach the weights necessary to keep the scope in the water. The weights themselves were rocks tied up in burlap bags, and the plan was to tie the burlap bags to the hoop and then throw the bags into the water. Marty had thought about the weights carefully, and in case he needed to attach more weights, he had extra ropes tied to the hoop.

The materials for the hydroscope had cost Marty about 24 dollars. Most of this—the PVC pipe and glue—he bought at the Home Depot in Brooklyn. The mirror was from his bathroom. His local coffee shop had given him the burlap coffee sacks that now held the rocks. The flashlight came from Walgreen's. It was guaranteed waterproof to 50 feet but it might not be of much use, as the water could be so murky. Also, once switched on and submerged, there was no way to switch it off without taking the hydroscope out of the water, and this might not be possible because the weights would be holding it down. Marty began to realize that the light and the mark II hydroscope would only good only good for one use.

Return to the Dead Zone

Before returning to the dead zone, Marty reminded Tanisha that he had helped her get to the airport to rescue geese. He then asked if she would go back with him to the dead zone to look deeper into the water for signs of life. She agreed.

The hydroscope was big but weighed only about 20 pounds. Once outside his apartment, Marty hoisted the hydroscope on his shoulder, wedging it against his neck, and holding it with his right hand he carried it to the bus stop.

That was where he planned to meet Tanisha. The bus stop was by a Payless shoe store on Flatbush Avenue with the Payless collection of multicolored plastic shoes. The shoe store customers shared the pavement with the queue for the bus; they eyed Marty and his hydroscope cautiously, fearful that it would swing and hit them. At the stop, Marty made his way to the front of the queue, as he thought that the bus driver would let him on with the hydroscope if there were a long line of passengers queued behind him. This didn't work. The bus door opened next to him and he would have been the first to get on, but the hydroscope got stuck in the bus's doorway between the handrail and the fare collection box.

"It's too big," the bus driver said.

"Can you open the rear door?" Marty asked.

The driver didn't answer, but the rear door opened. And Marty, without paying a fare, squeezed backward off the bus and towards the back door. As he hoisted the hydroscope onto the bus, he felt a hand behind him. And, expecting it was Tanisha's hand, was surprised to see that a very large man was helping him hoist the hydroscope onto the bus.

The back doorway was wide enough and the hydroscope did not get stuck, but Marty had to tilt his end down to it to get it up the stairs.

Once on the bus, Marty moved towards the back and took the seat facing across the bus over the rear wheel. Tanisha caught up and took the seat next to him. The large man followed and took the seat over the other wheel. Marty held the hydroscope between his knees, steadying it with his right hand. Marty said thanks to the man for helping and started to observe him. He silently guessed that the man was over six feet tall and weighed about 225 pounds—lean. He was missing one tooth, and it looked like his long hair had been straightened. The right side of his face bore a scar, and he constantly rubbed it. He also had a lip twitch that he seemed to be trying to control. Marty sensed from the jagged appearance of the scar that there had been much violence in the man's past.

Marty was surprised when the man pointed to the hydroscope and asked, "What have you got there?"

"A hydroscope," Marty replied.

The man leaned in towards Marty, touched the drainpipe, "That's a drainpipe," he said.

"I made it myself from pipes that I got from Home Depot," Marty replied.

"You should have gone to Lowe's."

Marty smiled but didn't reply. The man repeated, "You should have gone to Lowe's."

And when Marty again smiled and again didn't reply, the man started to talk to himself. He started by describing a meeting in Texas that took place in August 1950. It was in a bar outside of San Antonio. There were three people at the meeting and two of them were there to pick up some money. At the meeting, someone had a gun, someone had a knife, and for some reason that was never explained, someone had been disrespectful. He raised his right hand and used a slashing motion as he felt the scar on his face. Then he said, "Stop being disrespectful," over and over again. And with each repetition his voice got louder. As he got very loud, he moved his hand from his face and started banging on the bus seat. Marty shifted in his seat a little. Clearly, the man at the meeting had been knifed.

Tanisha moved towards the front of the bus, as did most of the other passengers at the back, but something about the man fascinated Marty, and he stayed. It wasn't the meeting to pick up the money, or the gun, or the knife, or the twitch, or the scar on his face. It was the fact that the event in Texas had stayed in the man's mind for 60 years. He was obsessed with it. Marty was also obsessed with an event that occurred 60 years ago. The event that Marty was obsessed with was the destruction of his childhood playground in Jamaica Bay.

Did the guy stay awake at night going over what had happened in Texas? Did the event ruin the guy's relationships with his friends? The guy obviously had been good looking at one point, but the prominent scar had changed that.

Just before the bus got to the Kings Plaza mall, the man turned to look forward and then pressed the bell to stop the bus.

As he got off the bus he turned towards Marty, "I don't like you," he said.

Marty, not sure what to say, shook his head.

Tanisha returned to the seat above the rear wheel, "Why didn't you move away like everyone else?" she asked.

"It's interesting that he's still obsessed with what happened in Texas 60 years ago," Marty replied.

"He needs to focus on what's happening now, and so do you. You're getting distracted. We need to focus on saving the geese at the airport and stop looking for life in the dead zone," Tanisha said.

"Maybe you are right, but sometimes I also obsess about the past. I obsess about what happened 60 years ago at the dead zone," Marty replied.

Marty and Tanisha stayed on the bus for three more stops and got off at the marina. He leaned the hydroscope against the marina's chain-link fence to take a breather, pulled out a bottle of water from his coat pocket, and took a drink. At some points, the creepers growing on the fence blocked the view, but you could see through it to the car park, the boats in silhouette, and then the still water of Dead Horse Bay.

It was a sunny, humid day with low-flying cumulus clouds. Marty put the hydroscope back on his shoulder and again held it in place with his right hand as he made his way down to his boat. He hadn't anticipated that the hydroscope wouldn't fit in the cabin, it was too big to lie across the boat, and he couldn't move about with it in the cockpit. He lashed it alongside the hull like a fish that was too big to haul on board. He took care with the ties to make sure that it would not go into the water. He then gave Tanisha a hand to get on board.

Tanisha sat down, "I hope that we're not going to have the same conversation about life vests that we had on the last trip," she said.

"What was that?" Marty asked.

"You told me to put on this life vest, but you are not wearing one," Tanisha said.

"Have you ever fallen overboard?" Marty asked.

"No," Tanisha replied.

"I've gone in the water twice. Once I fell overboard, and the second time I deliberately went into the water to see if I could climb back on board."

"Did you wear a life vest?"

"No, but I did get back on board both times."

"And me?"

"You wouldn't have made it." And, handing Tanisha a vest he said, "You have to wear a life vest."

Leaving the marina, Marty motored because he did not want the boat to heel and put the hydroscope under. Going under the Gil Hodges Memorial Marine Park Bridge, he noticed that the boat smelled of oil and gasoline, pretty much the same smell as the cars on the bridge. There was no wind to move the air and the smells hung around. The second bridge smelled the same, and just after it was a turn north towards Kennedy. Marty got his bearings not by the church spire or the breakwater that he had known as a kid, but by aircraft noise and the shadows of airplanes as they came in slowly to land.

As Marty brought the boat to a halt, Tanisha asked, "Why are we stopping here? It's the same place that we came to when we visited the airport at night.

"Yes, but we are not going ashore. We are going to look down into the water for any sign of life," Marty replied.

"Is this the dead zone?" Tanisha asked.

"Yes," Marty replied.

When Marty put the hydroscope in the water, it floated horizontally, resting on the water's surface. It was waterproof, but before he could use it, it had to hang vertically. Marty tied two burlap bags to the lower end of the hydroscope. After filling the bags with rocks, he tossed the bags into the water. The hydroscope began to sink, and with the addition of two more bags of rocks, it started to hang vertically.

With the flashlight on, Marty could see down to a depth of nine or ten feet. There was a reflection back from the flashlight like fog in a car's headlights. He watched black specs that seemed to be solid matter drift downward past his light. The light reflected off the solids, which shone like little stars falling.

"I can only see black specs falling," Marty said.

"Let me look," Tanisha said.

So they switched places. Marty moved to the center of the boat and Tanisha to the side, where she could look into the hydroscope.

"Something is moving near the edge of the circle of light," Tanisha said.

"What does it look like?" Marty asked.

"It's small, and shaped like a mushroom, and it has an opaque layer around the stem."

Marty took the scope back quickly and, peering in, he saw the gray shape drifting gradually down into the deep. He tried to turn the scope to get a better view, but the weights held it in place. The hydroscope only had a small field of vision.

Quickly removing his shirt, Marty jumped into the water and swam down to where he had seen the mushroom shape drifting. He could see a foot ahead and stretched out his hand further. He felt something soft and slimy—seaweed. He grabbed again, but there was nothing. He then remembered that objects under water appear closer than they actually are, and he started to go deeper. With hand outstretched, he felt a prickly sensation, and with his eagerness to get hold of it he almost squashed it. Bringing it to the surface, he held it towards the sun and saw the opaque layer around the stem and the delicate markings on the mushroom-shaped body. He wasn't sure if it was alive. How could he tell? He passed it to Tanisha and then realized that he would have a hard time climbing back onto the boat.

There was a ladder at the stern, but it did not reach down very far into the water. There was also a rope, and if he could grab it he could pull himself up until his feet were on the ladder.

He was cold and bruised on his chest when he got back on deck. The water had not warmed up from last winter. It reminded Marty of the times when he was a kid and gone into the water in June, only to endure a bout of shivering when he came out. His eyes half-closed, his tongue started to slowly lick the salty water off his lower lip. Marty grabbed a rag, the only cloth available, and used it as a towel to dry himself off.

Taking the small creature back from Tanisha he realized that he had nowhere to put it. He looked for a container in the cabin, but couldn't find one. Then he remembered that he had brought a sandwich in a plastic bag. He scooped up water into the bag and, noting that the bag did not leak, he dropped the small creature in it and tied a knot with the bag handles so that the water would not spill out.

"What is it?" Tanisha asked.

"I don't know," Marty replied.

"Is it what I saw moving towards the edge of the circle of light?" Tanisha asked.

"Yes," Marty replied.

Smelling sulfur on his body, Marty looked back. At age 10 he had played in Grassy Bay and visited the islands and the channel network north of Pumpkin Patch Channel. Back then, this had been marshland and the water was at most a few feet deep. There were rock pools with seaweed, tiny fish, skaters, dragonflies, and crabs. Back then, a 10-year-old could stand on the sandy bottom, which he often did when he took a break from swimming. The sulfur smell had come later, after the dredging created the stagnant pools.

The Jellyfish

"Jellyfish have drifted along on ocean currents for millions of years, even before dinosaurs lived on Earth."
—*National Geographic Kids*

Marty lived in a second-floor walk-up in Crown Heights, the entrance was dimly lit and led into a long, narrow kitchen that looked a lot like the cabin of an old wooden boat. The walls were off-white and the floor was a dull wood-colored linoleum tile. He'd made the kitchen cabinets and kitchen counter himself. They were sturdy, made from knotty wood, and roughly finished with several layers of varnish. The countertop was red tile

Once home, Marty poured the contents of his plastic bag into an enamel bowl that he placed on the kitchen counter. Looking carefully, he convinced himself that what he had was a jellyfish, but not a jellyfish that he was familiar with. Unsure if it would sting again, he put on kitchen gloves before trying to pick it up. The jellyfish was slippery and slipped from his hands. Taking off the gloves he tried again; when he touched the jellyfish, he felt the same prickly sensation that he felt when he first picked up the jellyfish, the prick was strong enough for Marty to realize that it was alive. With bare hands, the jellyfish really did feel like jelly, but it was not sticky or clingy like jelly usually is. It did have a gooey feeling, however. Pressing a little harder, he felt that the center was hard. Wondering how alive it was, as he had squashed it when he had caught it, he released his grip and poked it. Strangely, the fish did not try to move away, but the cap of the mushroom began to expand and contract. It seemed like it wanted to escape but could not control the direction in which it traveled.

This jellyfish didn't match the description of either of the two jellyfish that Marty knew. He knew the moon jellyfish, a milky saucer-shaped creature that, when washed up on shore, looked like a disk-shaped pad of hardened jelly. The moon jellyfish that Marty had seen were four or five inches in diameter. He'd also seen a sea nettle in Jamaica Bay. It had a bell shape and was semitransparent with small, white dots and reddish-brown stripes. The sea nettle was bigger than the moon jellyfish, the bell was maybe 24 inches across. The jellyfish in the enamel bowl had a two-inch cap with a stalk about three inches long. The cap consisted of a flattened disk, and the stalk had what looked like a mouth on the end. The color was subtle, opaque with a yellow tint.

Marty put the jellyfish and the water back into the plastic bag and walked with it to the main branch of the Brooklyn Public Library. He asked the librarian at the information booth about jellyfish, and he sent Marty upstairs to the natural history room.

In the natural history room, a librarian was sitting behind a desk. He was of middling build and middling all around. He was maybe in his late-40s or early-50s, with dark brown hair, thick spectacles, and a pencil held behind one ear. He wore a white shirt with rolled-up sleeves and a t-shirt underneath, tucked into shiny pants. A civil servant sort, he made a small smile when Marty approached.

"Excuse me, can you help me identify a jellyfish?" Marty said.

"Do you have a picture?" The librarian asked.

"No, but I have the fish with me in a bag," Marty replied.

The librarian peered inside the bag and took the pencil from behind his ear and poked the jellyfish with it before saying, "This is the first jellyfish I've seen in the library. Is it alive?"

"Yes, but it's not a moon jellyfish or a sea nettle," Marty replied.

"Where did you find it?"

"In Jamaica Bay, in an area known as the dead zone."

"We might have a book on jellyfish in the 970s, but it's dated. Feel free to browse if you like. Let me look online, it's shaped like a mushroom."

Marty thought that, unlike the cops that he had met when he had first gone to the dead zone, the librarian was helpful.

The librarian typed "mushroom-shaped jellyfish" into Google Chrome.

Opening the first link on the page, the librarian said, "Dendro-gramma." And he began to read from the article, "This oddball jellyfish may represent an early branch on the tree of life. It should perhaps be classified under its own phylum, separate from most known species. The organisms have a cylindrical stalk capped by a flat, semitrans-parent disk that houses visible channels branching outwards. These channels, which resemble tree-like diagrams known as dendrograms, are the basis for its scientific name—Dendrogramma."

"The article says that the Dendrogramma is really small, but your jellyfish is fairly big.

Marty moved the plastic bag that contained the fish closer to his body, as if he needed to protect it. He was happy that life was returning to the dead zone.

The librarian closed the browser's window, opened the next link, and after a pause, said, "The first article might be wrong. Here it says that it's a bract that a larger organism shed. It's not a new species, but it belongs to a class of floating jellyfish known as siphonophores, that are found along the Australian coast. Yours is a dirty yellow and a moon jellyfish might have shed it. It may have drifted on the incoming tide into the dead zone. A bract is like a chicken without a head, it will live for only a short period of time."

This set Marty thinking. If what the librarian said was true, the jel-lyfish was dying. There was no new life in what had been a marshland playground that he had known when he was a kid. There was just a rem-nant of something else that had been living. Everything in the dead zone was either dead or dying.

The California Widow

Marty was late to arrive, and his date, Betsey, asked him, "Did you have trouble finding Muriel's Café?"

"A little, I'm glad that you are still here," Marty replied, as he put the jar of tadpoles that he was carrying down on the bar.

Betsey stared at the jar before saying, "It's okay." Marty met her eyes as she continued, "It's good to see you again. Why did you bring tadpoles?"

"I'd meant to drop them off at home, but I was running late."

"Where did you get them?"

"From the pond."

"Why?"

"They won't survive in the wild."

Muriel's Bar was a French café and bar on First Avenue and Fifty-third Street in Manhattan. The bar was cozy, candlelit, and had a floral scent of lavender and vanilla. The far wall had shelves with a display of model boats, an actual boat fender, a collection of hard-backed books, and various pieces of pottery. For Marty, the downside was the nondescript French music coming out of the walls; he would have preferred silence, and if they had to have model boats as part of the décor, they shouldn't have been such obvious Chinese imports.

Marty's date was a 64-year-old widow from California whom he had met a few weeks back when he offered to help carry her laundry. She was five feet four—five feet six in the heels that she was now wearing—thin but not skinny, and she had short red hair. Marty had begun to think of her as the California widow. She had given him a photograph of herself when they first met, and for the past couple of weeks Marty had looked at it daily. There was something that he liked about the happy smile on her half-turned face. When they had first met, she described herself as having a high sex drive, and two weeks back Marty had been happy about this, but now, it occurred to Marty that this might be a problem. Marty had not had sex for several years.

The barman came over and interrupted Marty's thoughts: "What would you like to drink?" he asked.

"A beer," Marty answered, "What do you have on tap?"

"Did you look at the menu?" the barman asked.

Marty stared blankly at him, and then Marty looked at Betsey for help but he didn't get any. Marty noticed that she was drinking wine, and as she lifted her glass, she asked for another. Marty was about to ask for the same until Betsey opened the menu and pointed to the list of beers. Not being familiar with any of them, Marty pointed to the draft Allagash White from Maine, as he liked the way the name sounded.

Betsey then gave Marty a quizzical look, "Have you dated a lot?" she asked.

"No," Marty replied.

"Not at all?"

"There was this one woman—"

"I knew it. What was she like?"

"—She was from the Rockaways. She was sweet, but she had some rough edges. She was different. I went out there to meet her a few times, but the last time I went out to meet her she didn't turn up."

"What was her name?"

"Eloise. She had bad skin and would curse. She called her ex-husband a redneck."

"Where did you meet her?"

"At the bar on Beach 92nd Street, the Bungalow Bar. I had stopped there to have a beer. The bar has a great view of Jamaica Bay, but it's a dive."

"Did you date anyone else?"

"I did date a visiting nurse. She came to visit me after I sprained my ankle," said Marty.

"And?"

"We went out for a while after I got better."

"Why didn't it work?"

"She proposed to me on February 29th, 2008. A leap year."

"I bet that was a shock."

"I'd never been proposed to."

"You could have said yes. I always said yes."

"I didn't. She broke up with me soon after."

"What was she like?" asked Betsey.

"Five-foot-seven-inches tall, attractive, black, soft-spoken, and caring. She was an excellent nurse," replied Marty.

"You're not going to do any better."

And in a rare moment of inspiration, Marty replied, "I did meet you."

"Did you ever date online?"

"No."

"Good. I don't date men who date online. If a guy is online, he's talking to other women."

Marty wanted to forget his recent relationships. He'd dated for the past five years and had a series of fumbling relationships, none of which lasted. He didn't want to reveal this to Betsey. But he didn't want to lie. He was happy to remember the relationship that he had with his wife. She and Marty had been married for 18 years when she died, but truth be told, his relationship with his boat had lasted longer than any of his romantic relationships.

By now Marty was enjoying the Allagash White and was more receptive when the barman returned with a larger menu and asked, "Do you want to order food?"

"Let me look," Marty replied, and he took the menu.

"They have good burgers," Betsey said.

"I'm not that hungry."

"You should try a dessert. Today's special looks good, strawberry Frasier cake. It's chalked on the board behind the bar; it's a coconut macaroon pie with strawberries."

"It sounds good. I'll have one."

"I'll get the same."

The barman brought over the two elaborately decorated pasties and said, "*Bon appétit.*"

"*Merci*," Betsey said and bit off the strawberry and the mint decoration before she added, with her mouth full, "It's good. I only ever eat organic."

"You are right. It is good," said Marty, biting from the edge.

As the barman moved to the other end of the bar, Betsey leaned in towards Marty, pulling his coat to the side, and said, "In your photo you looked thinner. What have you got on under there?"

"I'm wearing layers," Marty replied.

"How many layers?" Betsey asked.

"Three," Marty replied.

"Let me see," said Betsey as she pulled up Marty's outer layer.

"It was cold by the water. I took a walk before I got the tadpoles."

"Who were you with?"

"I went alone. I like to be alone."

"You need to get a windbreaker. You would only need to wear one layer if you had a windbreaker." And pulling up the second layer, Betsey repeated, "Let me see what's under there."

Marty tried to push Betsey's hand away before she pulled up his third layer and found his bare tummy.

"You're skinny; you would look good if you dressed better."

Then Betsey pulled Marty's right hand towards her and held on to it. She looked at Marty's arm, "How did you get the cut?" she asked.

Marty paused, "On a nail," he replied.

"It's black and red and it might be infected. It needs to be taken care of," Betsey said.

Marty shifted on his seat, as he took his hand back and pulled his sleeve down to cover the cut. Marty, not wanting to show Betsey the cut again, used his left hand to pull back the clothing layers.

Betsey looked away from Marty and at the jar of tadpoles for a while before she said, "The tadpoles wriggle up to the top of the jar and they look at me. Can I take the jar off the bar?"

"They look at you?" Marty asked.

"Staring, they wriggle as they come up to the top of the jar but they never take their eyes off me."

"I poked a hole in the top of the jar to let in air. They sometimes come to the surface to breathe."

"I'll put them over by the window."

"Don't spill the water. It's not tap water. The tadpoles like the water from the pond."

Betsey moved the tadpoles very carefully and put them next to a jar of flowers on the window sill.

"How did you cut your arm?" Betsey again asked.

"I told you. I cut it on a nail."

"I don't believe you. Do you think that I was born yesterday?"

"I guess that I didn't sound too convincing. I was out at Kennedy airport with wire cutters, cutting holes in crates when I caught my arm on a sharp edge."

"If you told me what you are up to, it might help."

"I was out at Kennedy airport helping a friend rescue geese. They use the animal crates to cage the geese."

"You set the geese free?"

"No, the crates were empty. I cut the holes in the crates so that they could not use them."

"Did you talk to your friend about cutting the holes?"

"No."

"You're an old fool. Back in California, I joined a group that was trying to save some redwood trees. It was 1990, and they had organized a redwood summer. Who is caging the geese?"

"Wildlife Services, they don't help wildlife, they mostly kill it. The guy in charge of rounding up the geese is called Bill Bruford and he has a sidekick called Donny."

"The Yes Drummer?"

"No, not him"

"What do you know about him, apart from the fact that he does not play drums?"

"Not much."

"You need to study Bill Bruford and start to think things through. You are too impulsive; there was no point cutting holes in crates that can easily be replaced. Study his makeup and see how he operates. Is he a loner like you? Does he work well with Donny?"

"Is that all?"

"No, notice what he wears. Notice if it bothers him when he gets his clothes dirty."

"Why?"

"You will need to outwit him."

Marty took another bite from the edge of the strawberry Frasier cake before Betsey got up, "Excuse me, I'll be back," she said.

"Where are you going?" Marty called after her.

"To the bathroom. I'll be back," Betsey replied.

Marty listened to her heels on the wood floor as she headed along the bar towards the back of the restaurant. Hearing the clicking stop, Marty looked around and saw her talking to the barman. From the side, Marty saw the small bulge of her tummy. It was the cutest thing. She was wearing high-waisted, fitted pants made from a smooth, shiny black, synthetic fabric and a frilly white blouse. The pants were a tight fit and perfectly outlined the small bulge of her tummy; they had to have been custom-tailored.

When Betsey returned, Marty asked, "What did the barman have to say?"

"He asked me if I had noticed the new menu."

"I didn't know that you had been here before."

"I live nearby."

"What were you up to while I was gone?"

Marty shifted on his seat and did not want to admit that he'd been looking at her or that he'd noticed her tummy and thought that it was the cutest thing. Looking towards her, he was relieved to see that Betsey was not expecting an answer; she was smiling at him.

It was then that Marty remembered all the things that he had wanted to ask Betsey. He was curious about her move to New York, her job, and her dog.

"Why did you move to New York?" He asked.

"I got divorced. My first husband was artistic, he was charming and sweet, and like you, he was clueless about food and drink. I was 28 when I got married and I still have a picture of me in a white dress. Jimmy Carter won the presidency the same year. He was a wonderful man and, for me, it was a wonderful year."

"Who made it wonderful? Your first husband?"

"No. Jimmy Carter. There has not been anyone like him since. You know, had my first husband exercised and eaten well, he might still be alive today."

"Wasn't Jimmy Carter too liberal?"

"Not liberal enough for me. My first husband was a conservative, a macho man, and a womanizer, and I didn't like his womanizing. I could never orgasm with him and I think it was because I was silently fighting him.

Betsey then looked at Marty, as if she were asking for permission to continue, and Marty nodded his head

"My second husband was a cop. He didn't do anything much except sit at a desk and gossip. He was boring as hell. He took Viagra and was under the impression that it would make him a better lover. During sex, he would just pump, pump, and pump. I was 37 when he passed away. He didn't collapse on me during sex like I expected, he collapsed at his desk in the police station—he was laughing at something. The doctor said that he had a heart condition and, you know, I was shocked.

Betsey again paused, and Marty nodded again.

"My third husband was a television producer and he thought of me as a trophy wife. I can't believe that I ended up with him. He did have a great smile and he used it a lot, and that's what got me. There is no other explanation. I was 45 when he left me for a woman that he met at the television studio."

"Did you have to work after he left?" Marty asked.

"I had to get a job when my third husband divorced me. I had a daughter and he didn't support her, also I needed money for the divorce. At first, I mostly worked for friends doing interior design," Betsey replied.

There was a long pause, "How did you meet husband number three?" Marty asked.

"Number three came to the funeral of number two. They were friends from high school. But to answer your question, I wanted to get away from all the memories. That's why I moved to New York," Betsey replied.

"Why do you want to get married again?" Marty asked.

"I don't. Life is too short for mistakes. Gosh, is that the time? I have to run."

"But I have more questions; I was going to ask about your job and your dog."

"Another time."

Betsey then turned to kiss Marty on his cheek, and to his surprise, she also gave him a hug before saying, "I'll call you. Don't forget your tadpoles; they are over by the window."

Marty picked up the tadpoles and left the café a little after Betsey. To Marty, Betsey was too liberal, and she talked too much. But she was attractive, kind, and fun, and she had a gentle touch that he liked.

Marty Visits Howard Beach

Marty didn't want to go out to Howard beach to snoop on Bill Bruford, but he could see Betsey's reasons for wanting him to do it. He was thinking about this when he started to check out Bruford by taking the IND Rockaway Line out to the Howard Beach-JFK Airport stop. It was a late Saturday morning, and most of his fellow passengers were on their way to the airport. Getting off the train, Marty left the crowd as he turned east along 75th Road towards Cross Bay Boulevard. At the boulevard, Marty remembered what Tanisha had told him about the area. Back in the 1980s, a black guy had been murdered near here. A mob of white youths chased the guy across the boulevard onto the Belt Parkway, where a car hit him. Tanisha had heard about the incident at Brooklyn Law School, but what surprised Marty was that this was the only thing she knew about Howard Beach.

Marty had gotten Bruford's address from the Yellow Pages. Bruford had probably grown up in Howard Beach, gone to school there, and attended church. People did not move into Howard Beach; they grew up there.

Turning off the boulevard, he headed down the block towards Bruford's house. In the middle of the block, there was a guy with shears clipping a hedge. Marty said a quick hello to the guy before continuing to Bruford's house at the end near the water. There was a beware-of-the-dog sign on the gate. Over the fence, Marty saw a small yard and a freshly painted two-story house. There was a small dock but no boat. The house construction was wood-frame with vinyl siding and a gabled roof. It was on the water, concrete posts or stilts held it up, and there was a path on stilts leading up to the door. There was nobody outside, but the door was open. It was too dark, however, to see anything inside.

Surprisingly, Marty liked the house and the view, and his dislike for Howard Beach started to melt. The house had a great view of Jamaica Bay, a bay that Marty liked, and Marty could see why someone would want to live here.

Having no reason to knock on the door, Marty took another look over the fence, and then he stepped back and started to retrace his steps back towards Cross Bay Boulevard. Halfway down the block, the guy with the shears was still clipping the hedge. Marty crossed over to him and asked, "Do you know Bill Bruford?"

The guy turned and pointed back down the road, "He lives at the end."

"I've just come from there," Marty replied.

"He's usually home. Did you knock?" The guy said.

"No," Marty replied.

"You should have. It's funny, I didn't see him last weekend, there was a block party, and the whole block was out."

"Is he married?"

"I think he married his cousin."

"Can you do that?"

"Well, maybe his second cousin. It happens in Howard Beach."

The guy then returned to clipping the hedge. Marty stood around for a few minutes hoping to get the guy's attention again, but when this didn't happen Marty moved on.

Further down the block, an older guy was walking a dog. Remembering the beware-of-the-dog sign outside Bruford's house, Marty went up to the dog walker, looked at the guy's dog, and asked, "Do you know Bill Bruford?"

"He has a dog that he got from the pound," the guy replied.

"Do you ever talk to him?"

"He keeps to himself."

The dog pulled against the leash and the dog walker moved off.

Disappointed, Marty headed back to Cross Bay Boulevard, or "the boulevard" as it's known, and crossed the six-lane highway that bisects Howard Beach. Marty noticed that on both sides of the highway the people were predominantly white, there were poorer people on the other side of the highway and richer people on this side, but if his experiences with the hedge cutter and dog walker were anything to go by, they all knew each other. Down the highway a little further, Marty went into a clam bar, sat on one of the polished wooden chairs at the bar, and ordered a scotch. There was a television tuned to a sports channel on the nearest wall, and a picture of a boxer whom he didn't recognize was next to it.

Returning with the drink, the barman said, "You're not from around here."

"How do you know?" Marty replied.

"I know most people from around here," the barman said.

"I came here looking for a guy," Marty replied.

"What's his name?"

"Bill Bruford."

"He's a little league coach. There's a team picture on the far wall."

Marty walked over to the picture and asked. "Which one?"

"The one at the far end."

Marty studied the picture. Bruford was built, clean-shaven, and was wearing a t-shirt and a baseball cap. He had four or five muscles bulging out from his upper arm. It was hard to tell his age, he could be 30, 40, or 50.

"How old is the picture?" Marty asked.

"There is probably a date on it and there is a list of names on the brass plate at the bottom," the barman replied.

Marty waited until the barman looked away and then took a quick photo of the picture with his cell phone.

Delighted with his photo, Marty thought about asking the barman about Bruford's sidekick Donny. But then he thought better of it. It was possible that the barman knew Bruford well and Bruford might see a work connection if he found out that someone had asked about him and Donny. Trying to relax, Marty had a second whiskey at the bar but didn't get any more information from the barman except for the location of Bruford's home field. Marty slipped out of the bar when it started to fill up and the barman got busier.

The picture didn't amount to much except that now he would be able to recognize Bruford if he saw him. Also, it was hard to see how what he'd learned about the guy would help them frustrate the goose round-ups. Bruford was a clean-cut, muscular guy, and it was unlikely that he'd willingly get dirty. The guy was a loner who coached little league and had taken in a stray dog. Marty had not found what he expected. To all intents, Bill Bruford was a quiet guy who kept himself to himself and who lived in a neighborhood that Marty was starting to like.

Marty Falls in Love

When Marty returned to Muriel's, he was surprised when the guy at the door recognized him, and even more surprised when the guy at the door said, "Betsey's at the bar, towards the back."

Betsey was wearing a knee-length, silky, pink dress, but her hair had changed since the last time they met. It was now short, blow-dried red—or maybe orange—and purple. Glancing at the mirror over the bar, he noticed that they had removed the strawberry Frasier cake special from the menu and replaced it with peach tart. Betsey's appearance made Marty feel a little uncomfortable, as he was wearing the same coat that he'd worn the last time they met.

"The guy at the door recognized me," Marty said.

"I told him that you were coming," Betsey replied.

She greeted him with a smile, a kiss on the cheek, a "How have you been?" and "Did you check out Bill Bruford?"

Sitting at the bar next to her, Marty noticed her smiling reflection in the bar's mirror but he looked straight at her. He skipped her first question and smiled back as he answered the second question with, "Checking out Bill Bruford was creepy."

"Spill the beans," Betsey said.

"He lives in a house by Jamaica Bay. I wouldn't mind living there myself," Marty replied.

"What did you find out?"

"He's a loner."

"Loners aren't usually in charge. Are you sure?"

"Yes, I talked to two of his neighbors and they both said the same thing, it's a long story. Let me get a drink," and Marty quickly got a drink from the bar.

"Is he married?" Betsey asked.

"To his cousin."

"Is that legal?"

"It's legal in New York State."

"Anything else?"

"I got a photo of him."

"How?"

"It's from a team photo that was hanging on the wall of the bar."

"What team?"

"He coaches little league."

"Let me see it."

"It's not very clear. It's a photo of a photo," and Marty opened his phone and showed Betsey the picture of Bill Bruford with the little league team.

"Is he the clean-cut big guy at the back?"

"Yes, the names are listed along the bottom. He's the second from the left at the back. I would not have known if his name was not on the brass plate."

"He looks good."

"He's the coach. I'd had asked about him at the clam bar, and the barman told me about the photo."

"He looks like a nice guy."

"Yes, and it's giving me a problem."

Marty knew that Bruford looked like a nice guy, but he did not want to hear it. In his mind, he always pictured Bruford as a villain who gassed geese. Maybe there were two sides to the guy—a Dr. Jekyll and a Mr. Hyde; the double personality was preferable to the nice guy image. Marty had also thought that Howard Beach would be a horrible place, as he had heard bad things about it for years, but it was not. The small, clapboard houses wedged against the water presented a picturesque view, and with the light bouncing off the water the place was magical. He had also thought that he would feel insecure there, but instead he felt welcome.

Now that his perceptions had changed, it was getting harder for Marty to deal with Bruford.

Betsey may have read some of Marty's thoughts as she said, "You still have to outwit him. He may be a nice guy, but you have to outwit him if you are going to save the geese."

"How?" Marty asked.

"You haven't much to go on. You should go back," Betsey replied.

Marty switched from looking at Betsey directly and started to watch her in the bar's mirror as he said, "I don't want to go back. I don't want to be known in the area."

"Known by who?"

"Well, nobody really. I only met a couple of his neighbors, but we did not exchange names."

"You should get a look inside Bruford's place."

"Why"

"You can learn a lot from looking inside someone's house."

"My eyes were adjusted to the bright sunlight and I could not see inside."

"You could have knocked on his door and tried to sell him something. Stand close to the door out of the sunlight, and when he answers you should be able to look inside."

"You were going to tell me about your job," Marty said.

"Later. I want to tell you something else first," Betsey replied.

"What?" Marty asked.

"Do you know that I almost turned around and left when we met last week?" Betsey replied.

"No."

"You do remember what you were wearing? What you were carrying?"

"The tadpoles?"

"Yes, and the baggy layers under the coat. Do you remember me checking them out?"

"Yes," Marty said, taking a long drink of beer.

"You know I only stayed because you seemed so helpless."

"Helpless?"

"You had difficulty ordering a beer."

"Mostly when I get a beer, it's a Miller or a Bud. I didn't know there was a beer menu."

"You made a bad impression."

"I did apologize for being late, and I was embarrassed about the layers."

"You're a wiz at understatement. I have friends who come here and they notice what I wear and who I'm with. I work as an interior designer, and I meet some of my customers here. It will be hard to sell interior design if I'm dating someone who is scruffy."

Marty felt terrible, he turned away from Betsey and the mirror. His world was falling apart. Last week, he'd looked at Betsey's photo almost daily, and he had looked forward to seeing her at the end of the week. He did not know what to say. He realized that what she was saying was true, but he did not know how to respond. He should have taken the tadpoles home first. Plus, he'd had the same experience before with his clothes. The lady from the Rockaways, Eloise, whom he'd dated before Betsey, made similar comments about his clothes. Well, not exactly the same thing, she had criticized his hair and called his jacket a rag. It was a dilemma because Marty had always felt that dressing well didn't matter, but now it might. His best friend from college had looked down on people who dressed well, and Marty followed his example. Marty continued to look down on people who dressed well long after he had lost track of his best friend.

Still unsure how to respond, Marty felt a tear start to make its way down his cheek, and he was trying to figure out how to hide it when Betsey leaned in and wiped it away with her finger. Betsey's wipe had the surprising effect of causing Marty to tear up more.

"I like your sensitivity. It's unusual in a man," Betsey said.

"I hadn't intended to tear up. It just happened," Marty replied.

"You look anything but sensitive, but you are sensitive. None of my husbands were sensitive," Betsey said.

Marty knew that he had revealed himself with the tears. By now, Betsey probably knew that he liked her, but what else had she figured out? He was about to tell Betsey that he liked her when she interrupted him.

"You still look sad," Betsey said, and she held onto the bar and leaned into Marty and kissed him on the lips, "Does that feel better?" she asked.

Marty wanted to kiss her back, but he chose not to, as it seemed inappropriate to kiss back after being kissed better. The kiss tasted like honeysuckle and vanilla. He ran his tongue on the inside of his lips to savor it. He did feel better, but he delayed expressing himself as he moved his stool in, towards her.

Betsey looked at him, and he could have sworn that she had a pitying look, "Do you feel better?" she again asked.

"Yes. Is there another kiss?" Marty asked.

"You're getting fresh."

"I feel close to you."

"Let me get you a stiff drink. There might be another kiss later." Betsey got the barman to come over and pour Marty a whiskey by shouting, "He needs a whiskey."

Sipping the whiskey, Marty got an inkling that a relationship with Betsey could work. Betsey did kiss Marty again, and this time he felt that Betsey was genuinely sorry. Marty started to show the smile that he had suppressed earlier. And slyly he watched for Betsey's reaction in the mirror above the bar.

"I love your smile. It's both innocent and unfathomable. You also have beautiful blue eyes," Betsey said.

"Did you set me up?" Marty asked.

"I don't know what you mean," Betsey said.

"You are not as innocent as you look. You played me. When we last met, you were not going to turn around and leave," Marty said.

Marty's Doubts

The next time that Marty met Betsey, he decided not to get on the subway at his local stop but to walk to the next stop before getting on the train. Often, when his mind was not clear, Marty would take a walk. A walk usually helped to clear his thoughts. The walk took him through Prospect Park to the subway station at Grand Army Plaza.

Entering the park at the Flatbush Avenue entrance, Marty had little idea about what was bothering him. He had an hunch that it was the recent closeness with Betsey, but it could have been something else. On the downhill, his shoelaces flopped loosely against his ankles, but he didn't stop to tie them because he did not want to lose his pace. He felt a curious link between his mind and feet. If his feet kept going, this would be a good time to think.

For Marty, the mornings were best, because early in the day his leg did not bother him. A foot pronation had left him with some pain and a slightly comical walk. He was aware of this, and sometimes he looked down to watch as his right foot turned inward every fourth step.

As he turned towards Grand Army Plaza, he had to walk uphill. On the hill, Marty felt his heart start to pump faster, it was circulating more blood not just to his muscles but also to his brain. This should be the best time to figure out what was bothering him. It had to be Betsey, as there was little else that had changed during the past week.

Marty was a little out of breath when he got to Long Meadow, and he was glad for an excuse to take a rest. He paused to take in the view of the upper field. It looked greener after the recent rain. Large trees bordered it, as did the buildings on the north side of the park. Looking up, he saw a few kites. It was a good place to fly a kite; it was open and the wind blew in from all sides. Here, there was space to let his mind spread out, but he needed to concentrate and stop the drift. Feeling the wind against his face and the soft grass against his ankles made concentration more difficult. He needed to focus on Betsey.

After he had crossed Long Meadow, Marty was starting to resent how Betsey was trying to change him. It seemed like she was taking charge of his life. She was choosing his clothes, had switched his diet, and had tried to get him to put down larger tips. Betsey was also the reason he had taken that trip to Howard Beach to find out more about Bill Bruford. It turned out that Bill Bruford had a good side, and this bothered Marty. It was easier to deal with an anonymous evil figure than it was to deal with a coach who was in charge of a little league team.

Leaving the park at Grand Army Plaza, Marty took the circle to the subway and got on a Manhattan-bound train. He walked down the car until he got a seat between two kids who knew each other, but not well enough to move over. He had figured out why Betsey was bothering him but not how to deal with it. He stewed on this for a bit, and then he opened his newspaper and turned to the sports section.

Arriving at Muriel's Bar without a plan, Marty was not looking forward to Betsey's positive and warm manner. Once inside, he walked along the bar towards the back of the café. When Betsey got up from her stool to give him a hug, Marty stepped aside to avoid it. He wasn't feeling affection; there was a mismatch. Marty was a little angry, and Betsey was her usual affectionate smiling self.

"What's wrong? Don't you like me anymore?" Betsey asked.

"I'm just a bit mad. It's not you," Marty replied. But it was.

"Then what is it?" Betsey asked.

"Can we go somewhere else?" Marty said.

"I like it here."

"People know us here, and they listen in."

"I'm comfortable."

"I'm not. Muriel's is too upscale. It's too posh."

"It's not."

"We never go anywhere else." Marty wished he'd taken the time on the train to figure out what he needed to say to Betsey. He would have had a plan if it had come to him after the walk. He continued, "I can't go on like this."

"Whatever is wrong?" Betsey said.

"I'm used to getting my own way," Marty said.

"And you don't anymore? I only tried to smarten you up a bit so that I can take you to nice places," Betsey said.

"I'm too old to change."

"You're only as old as you think you are. You must be afraid of the sex."

"It's two years since I had sex, but I haven't forgotten how to."

"You need to get laid."

"I'm breaking up with you"

"You didn't want to stay around long enough to get laid?" And she laughed.

Was she laughing at him? Marty thought so.

"I have to go," Marty said. And he left her at the bar.

He felt funny as he left. That morning, to increase the likelihood of sex Marty bought condoms at the pharmacy. To disguise the purchase, he also bought three other items: Morning Freshness mint soap, Amarelli licorice toothpaste, and an Oral B toothbrush. He left with soap, toothpaste, the toothbrush, and condoms.

Fighting for Love

Marty went to bed early that night, but he did not sleep well. His window was open so he could hear some street noise—car doors closing, people shouting goodnight. Nothing that he wouldn't normally sleep through, but it took a long time for him to turn his head away from the street noise and fall asleep. He woke up later facing the window, and the street noise was still there. He had clenched his teeth on the left—some of his teeth on the right were missing. Then he remembered that he had broken up with Betsey and the tension made sense. Waking up again, this time facing the ceiling, he was now glad that he had broken up. He got up, had a couple of glasses of beer to celebrate, and relaxed. Later, the drink took effect and he fell back asleep until his alarm went off at eight. The back of the room was still in darkness, and now he felt bad about breaking up. Would she take him back? He had little to go on. It was, however, going to be hard to start another day without her.

Marty usually resisted putting on a suit, but if he was going to get Betsey back it would help. His suit was double-breasted, dark blue with white pinstripes. Trying to look a little soft, a little feminine, he matched it with a lilac-and-gray shirt. He tried on a tie, but he didn't like the knot so it came off. He wiped the dust off his black wingtips and tied their shoelaces neatly with double bows.

He'd never been to Betsey's apartment, but it seemed easy enough to find. He knew where Muriel's café was, and from the café it was a short walk to Betsey's. She'd told him two weeks back, when they were in the café, that her building was on the next block and that it was the four-story building with the blue window frames. Assuming that he had an uphill battle to get Betsey back, he picked up a dozen red roses on the way. He did find her building without a problem, and when he got there he pressed her intercom button. He heard Betsey ask, "Who is it?"

"It's Marty," He replied.

There was silence for a few minutes until Betsey replied, "What do you want?"

"Can I come in?" Marty asked.

"Why?" Betsey asked, on the intercom.

"I want to talk," Marty replied.

Betsey didn't reply but Marty could hear movement over the intercom and then footsteps until Betsey opened the door. In the doorway, Betsey blocked Marty's entrance while Marty nervously moved his weight from foot to foot.

"We need to talk," Marty said, stepping back.

"We?"

"I need to talk to you."

"You need to apologize."

"I do?"

"You can't jerk me around like this," Betsey said.

Marty again shifted his weight.

"Well?" Betsey asked.

"I'm sorry."

"Is that a vintage or a revival look?" Betsey asked as she looked at Marty, up and down.

"It's a blue pinstripe that I bought a few years back." And he handed Betsey the roses.

"Thank you."

"Is there something wrong with the suit?"

"You actually look good, and the flowers are special, but your suit is old. You would look better if you bought a new one. Come in," Betsey said, and she stepped back from the door.

She then led Marty up the curved stairs to the second floor of the spacious pre-war building. Unlocking the apartment door, Betsey led him down a wide corridor past the kitchen and dining room and then continuing before they entered the living room. The living room had red décor and the curtains were closed, but two large lamps lit the room well. Betsey sat on the armchair and motioned for Marty to sit opposite her.

"Why did you change your mind about breaking up?" she asked.

"I made a mistake. I need you," Marty said.

"If we get back together, you have to agree to stop spending so much time alone with your own thoughts," Betsey said.

"I always think things out too much," Marty said.

"You need to visit your local bar and socialize, watch television, or read a book."

Betsey then moved to the sofa and was no longer facing Marty. From the side, Marty saw the small bulge of her tummy. He remembered it from when they first dated. It was the cutest thing.

Marty couldn't figure out how to comment on the bulge, "You look good," he said.

She did, she was wearing high-waisted, gray flannel pants and a pale blue blouse. The pants were a skin-tight fit and perfectly outlined the small bulge of her tummy.

"Would you like something to drink?" Betsey asked.

"A glass of water would be great," Marty replied.

She returned with a pitcher of iced seltzer water with lime and mint.

Marty took a drink, and despite the fact what he would have preferred tap water he smiled at the overkill, "Thank you," he said.

"You're welcome. You know that I like you too," Betsey said, moving closer.

"What do you like about me?" Marty asked.

"Don't be offended, but I love how you double-nod your head while you are concentrating. I love to hear you say "err, err" in every sentence when you are thinking what you are going to say. I love to see your right leg turn inward every fourth step. I love your long lean body and your soulful eyes. It's true; every bread has its cheese," replied Betsey.

"That's not all true," Marty said.

"Sure it is. Come sit nearer to me," Betsey said.

Betsey then put her hand out towards Marty and Marty took it, he concentrated on the way her skin felt against his hand.

Betsey then put both of her hands out and took a firm hold on Marty's hands before pulling him up "Let's go out and get lunch," she said.

But instead of turning towards the corridor and the outside door Betsey turned towards her bedroom, put on soft music, and started to undress.

Marty read the move but he held back a bit.

Betsey chided him, "You told me that you had not forgotten how to make love."

The Goslings

Marty wanted to do something about the geese roundup that had taken place at Prospect Park Lake last summer. He planned to attend the protest next month, but he also wanted to do more.

He'd get new geese to replace the geese rounded up in Prospect Park. He'd take them to the lake in Prospect Park. He might even be able to imprint himself on the replacements and get them to walk down to the lake.

Pio Pio Live Poultry in Brooklyn sold live chickens, live ducks, and animal feed but didn't sell geese. They didn't plan to. There was no call for geese.

But Marty's mother had told him that there was more than one way to skin a cat.

Marty's neighbor, Chris, who lived on the block, kept chickens. He bought day-old baby chickens online from Stromberg's Chicks and Game Birds. Chris was pretty sure that Stromberg's also sold geese.

From Stromberg's website, Marty discovered that Stromberg's sold goslings, not geese. Stromberg's minimum order for goslings was six. So, Marty bought six unsexed goslings. People usually bought domestic goslings to raise for their eggs or for eating. At Stromberg's, unsexed goslings were cheaper than sexed goslings, but with unsexed goslings, there was a chance that all the goslings would be the same sex.

Two days after he placed his order, the post office called and asked Marty to pick up his chicks. The goslings were in a box labeled "baby chicks," and he could see them as they moved against the air holes in the box. He could also hear a faint cheeping coming from the box. He was expecting a bigger package, so before he left the post office, his curiosity got the best of him, and he opened the box a little to look inside. The six goslings were fine. Marty closed the box and headed home.

Marty's Crown Heights apartment was a second-floor walk-up, it was long and narrow, a railroad apartment. The entrance led into a kitchen that in turn led into a living room, which was the middle room, and beyond the living room was his bedroom. The bedroom was the only room with a window and a view; the rest of the apartment was dimly lit. To the side of the kitchen was a bathroom, and at the back and to the side, a small, second bedroom that he used as an office. In the living room, there was a small hexagonal table with a television on it. Next to the table there was a settee, also a bookcase with a couple of books.

The kitchen looked a lot like the cabin of an old wood boat. It was long and narrow and cramped and there was a lot of wood. The walls were off-white and wood-grained linoleum tiles covered the floor.

As there was no room on the kitchen counter for the box of chicks. Marty put the box down on the table in the living room next to his television. Sitting down on the settee, he didn't switch on the television but watched the goslings through the holes in the box. Not quite sure what to do next, he got a beer from the fridge and began to drink it while pulling up a box corner to get a better look inside.

The goslings' fluffy down was light-brown to golden-yellow. Some of them made a quiet chirping sound, sounding a little like mice. They had tiny black bills, which served as both nose and mouth. They had glimmers in their eyes, which Marty saw as intelligence and love. Each seemed to have a distinct personality. When Marty put his hand in the box and watched carefully, it was always the same gosling that came to greet it, and the rest always moved away. Cathy, who worked at Buster's, had said that ducks didn't have personalities, but if ducks and geese were the same in this regard, she was wrong.

Later Marty made a larger box for the goslings by taping together two cardboard boxes that he had picked up at the supermarket. To make the goslings comfortable, he put a layer of wood shavings in the box. Still, the box was a little smaller than he would have liked. As he moved each gosling into the larger box, he could feel its heartbeat, and when he put the gosling down, he noticed how it ran to join the other goslings in the box to huddle together for warmth. Marty was extremely gentle the first time that he touched each gosling to start the imprinting process.

To ensure that the goslings had water, Marty cut small holes, but large enough for the goslings to put their heads through, into the sides of a plastic bottle. For the first feed, Marty soaked instant Quaker oats in water until he had a soup. For heat, he clipped a 60-watt work light to the side of the box. The heat from the light kept the box warm.

Satisfied with his work, Marty undressed and went to bed in the front room. He was tired, but there was a constant peeping from the goslings. Were they calling him? Had he already imprinted himself on them? He got out of bed and walked to the living room, and the peeping got quieter. It almost stopped when he sat on the settee and put his hand in the gosling's box. When he felt a gosling with his hand, he picked it up and put it down on his chest. The gosling seemed to like this and seemed like it was about to fall asleep. It was making a humming, almost a purring noise; it was a night-time sound like "peewee." The gosling seemed content, not flailing or struggling at all. Marty waited until the gosling was quiet and perfectly still before he put it back in the box. For his part, Marty took a while to fell asleep. He was tired, and it was now quiet, but he was uncomfortable on the settee, which was too short for his six-foot frame.

Hours later, Marty woke up late, knowing that he was going to have to continue to play father goose. He was going to have to imprint himself on the goslings, get them used to his voice, get them to walk in a line behind him, and attach them to his smell. To get them used to his voice, he talked to himself as he made breakfast. To get them attached to his smell, he dropped one of his dirty shirts into the goslings' box.

The next day when Marty got up from the settee (he had again slept next to the goslings), he remembered that he had names for the goslings. He'd stayed in bed that morning, awake and thinking, and had come up with three names: Pink, Puff, and Pickle. Pink for the gosling with a pink feather on its right side. Puff for the gosling with the orange and brown feathers that puffed out. And Pickle for the gosling that didn't bunch up with the others and mostly didn't seem to know what to do. This gosling was in a pickle. Pink always came up to him when he put his hand in the box, Puff kept a distance, and Pickle was all over the place.

It wasn't always easy to tell Pink, Puff, and Pickle apart. Pink had only a touch of pink on one feather and sometimes all the goslings looked puffy. And Pickle wasn't the only gosling to look lost. To sort things out, Marty began by cutting long and short pieces of colored wool. He planned to tag the goslings by tying small pieces of colored wool to their legs. Pink got a short piece of pink wool around one leg, Puff got yellow and brown wool, and Pickle got turquoise wool. He chose turquoise for Pickle because it seemed to signal indecision. Pink playfully tried to nibble the turquoise wool as Marty tied it around Pickle. The remaining three goslings had no tags.

Later, Marty took the goslings out of the box and lined them up in his kitchen near the entrance to his apartment. He wasn't going to walk them out of the apartment, he was going to walk them through the narrow kitchen to the front bedroom. Pink was first in line because Pink always came to the front of the box when he put his hand into it. The goslings closed in on each other, tidying the line that Marty made so that there was a uniform space between each gosling. After they shuffled around a bit, Marty took his place at the head of the line.

Marty quietly said, "Up, one-two, one-two …" and started to walk towards the front bedroom.

Marty heard the footsteps on the linoleum behind him as the goslings instinctively waddled behind him in single file. They saw Marty as a dad, and dads were to be followed. Marty looked around and saw that the leader was still Pink, but Pickle had not moved. For now, Marty ignored Pickle and continued with just the five.

It took a while to get to the front of the apartment, as the birds were small and could only take small steps. At the front, Marty turned and the goslings stopped. Marty stopped, stamped his foot, started off again saying, "Up, one-two, one-two …" but the goslings would not follow. Marty thought about this. Maybe their refusal to go back was logical, and anyway, when a gosling didn't want to do something, it wouldn't do it. So Marty gave up, put the goslings back in the box, and went back to the apartment entrance to get Pickle.

The next time that they walked, Marty dressed up to get Pickle to walk with him. He put on a black neck warmer and wound a white scarf around his head, so that, from their perspective, his head could pass for that of a Canada goose. The goslings didn't yet have the distinctive coloration of the Canada goose, which has a neck that looks as though a long black sock had been pulled over it. They also didn't have the Canada goose's band of white that extends up from the chin to behind each eye. But Marty's dress-up didn't work. Pickle still would not follow him. Pickle was neither mature nor imprinted.

Marty improvised a harness and a leash for Pickle using Velcro sewn to a piece of webbing and a length of string. The harness fastened around Pickle's body, not around his neck, where it would make breathing difficult for Pickle. The next time they walked, Marty would put the harness and leash on Pickle and pull him along with the other birds.

Marty wondered if Pickle was the most confused or the least confused gosling. But it probably didn't matter. Five goslings would follow him willingly. Pickle would walk on the leash.

The Vale of Cashmere

The Vale of Cashmere, in Brooklyn's Prospect Park, received its name from Irish romanticist Thomas Moore's 1817 poem "Lalla Rookh," a celebration of botany and romance in the Mughal Imperial Court.

You've got to give it to Brooklyn in New York, it's got both a Taj Mahal and a Vale of Cashmere. The Taj Mahal is a family-owned restaurant on Fifth Avenue that sells a large selection of Indian food, and the Vale of Cashmere is a natural valley at the northwest corner of Prospect Park.

The Vale of Cashmere was the unofficial locus of gay cruising in Brooklyn, and it's the place that Marty chose to hide the goslings after they got to be too big for his apartment. The gay men wanted to keep their cruising for sex hush-hush, and Marty wanted to keep the goslings hush-hush. The Vale of Cashmere was a good hiding place.

When the goslings were two weeks old, 12 inches tall, and too big for Marty's apartment, he decided it was time to move them out and house them somewhere else before he walked them down to the lake in Prospect Park. They were growing up, they didn't feel soft anymore, they were growing darker wing and tail feathers. Their voices were also transitioning from peeping baby sounds to their hoarse and raspy adult voices.

The Vale of Cashmere wasn't Marty's first choice for the goslings. He's asked his neighbor if he would house the goslings in an old chicken coop that he had in his backyard. The neighbor declined, explaining that geese were outlawed in New York City backyards and that the city would cart them away if they discovered them. Even so, the neighbor offered to give Marty his chicken coop and suggested that Marty hide the goslings in the park. A few days later, Marty discovered the Vale of Cashmere— the best place in the park to hide the goslings.

The chicken coop made it to the Vale of Cashmere through a hole in the fence on a quiet stretch of Flatbush Avenue. Marty dragged it away from the road, up a dirt path, and hid it in a hollow under some trees. He knew that few people ever came to this part of the park, and he'd seen how it had turned into a forest crisscrossed by dirt paths. Park management didn't maintain this part as well as they did the rest of the park. The only other people that Marty saw in the vale were a group of dirt bikers. They had made humps of dirt on the paths for ramps, which they jumped over on their bikes.

The chicken coop had a floor, three sides, a roof, and one window covered with chicken wire netting. The fourth side was missing, and in the neighbor's backyard it opened the coop to an outdoor run. Marty placed the chicken coop on bricks to keep it off the ground. He then hammered sticks into the ground and strung chicken wire over them to make an outdoor enclosure. There was a ramp leading down from the coop. The whole thing would be quite snug after he covered it with small branches.

The interior of the chicken coop was square, and Marty placed the goslings' water bowl in the center. He clipped a heat lamp to one wall, and on the opposite wall he attached a colored picture of the lake in Prospect Park. There was also a feeder, as the goslings were growing quickly and they ate a lot. Marty ran an extension cord from a nearby lamppost to power the heat lamp. The cord ran into the base of the lamppost, where Marty connected it to the wires that powered the lamp.

Marty used a children's set of watercolors to paint the picture of Prospect Park Lake. He had grass in the foreground, Prospect Park Lake in the middle ground, and the sky in the background. There was a duck on the lake and a single cloud in the sky. He used push-pins to secure the picture to the wall of the coop and hoped that the picture would imprint the lake on the goslings.

The goslings made it to the Vale of Cashmere through the same hole in the park fence that Marty had used to move the chicken coop. He carried them in their cardboard box to the hollow and moved them one by one from the box to the coop. At first, they seemed upset by the move, but they adjusted to it within the hour. They were happy because the feeder had gosling starter feed, and the open area of the coop had a pile of dandelions and groundsel, which Marty had cut. There were a lot of dandelions growing in the dry lily pools in the northern part of the vale.

That night, Marty stayed with the goslings until it was almost dark. He was reluctant to leave them, so before he set off for home, he took off a sock and dropped it into the coop so that they would remember him. Then he made his way through the vale to exit the park at Grand Army Plaza. When he got home, his apartment was empty and there was not much to do except switch on the television, which sat next to the empty gosling box. He'd visit the goslings tomorrow, take them more dandelions and groundsel from the disused lily ponds. He'd visit the goslings every day in the Vale of Cashmere until they were big enough to follow him down to Prospect Park Lake.

Prospect Park

On March 26, 2011, Tanisha phoned Marty to invite him to a goose protest that afternoon in Prospect Park. The protest event was called "Hands Around the Lake." They arranged to meet up by the Prospect Park Lake on a grassy area near the Well House. To get there, Marty entered Prospect Park by Vanderbilt Street and Prospect Park Southwest.

Staring to the north, Marty was looking for Tanisha when a short, stocky guy with long black hair and a beard emerged from the group and asked him loudly, "Are you from the Parks Department?"

It was Don. Marty recognized him instantly and started to laugh, even though Don seemed more subdued than when they last met. No American-flag bandana and bib overalls this time. Instead, Don wore a rugged-looking oil-cloth jacket, gray corduroy pants, and a baseball cap. Marty also noticed a look, one that he'd seen before in Don. It was a look that said, "I'm a little stupid and I'm not to be messed with."

"No," Marty replied.

"Are you waiting for someone?" Don asked.

"Tanisha," Marty replied.

"She told me that she had invited you," Don said.

"It's good to meet you again," Marty said.

"Did you sign the Goose Watch petition to save the mute swans?"

"No."

"Did you add your name to the petition to save elephants?"

"No"

"Did you support the campaign to save the Staten Island wild turkeys?"

"I didn't."

"Our New York State ballot initiative?"

"No."

"Our action to fight against invasive species?"

"No."

Don then slapped Marty on the back, "Then you're a goose-only guy," he said.

"That's right! I only support geese."

"Good for you! I'll talk to you again after the speeches," Don said.

Marty hadn't paid much attention to the slaughter of geese that had taken place in Prospect Park a year back. It had occurred before he'd met Tanisha and before she told him what was going on. Parting from Don, Marty took a place near the front of the crowd.

State Senator Eric Adams (Democrat, Park Slope) spoke first: "It's arrogant for humans to believe this planet was made just for humans," he said, prompting a spirited, "That's right!" and "Yes!" from the crowd. "These birds give us more than what we give them; we have an obligation and a responsibility to protect them.

"When the slaughter of innocent geese and goslings occurred in July of last year, I was both horrified and angered. I was dismayed by the manner in which these majestic creatures were killed. I am pleased to be in attendance at today's 'Hands Around the Lake' event to send a clear signal to those responsible for last year's massacre that the annihilation of innocent and defenseless wildlife will not be tolerated."

Adams then recalled "courting his first love" while gazing at Prospect Park geese.

Councilwoman Letitia James (Democrat, Fort Greene) spoke next, confessing the squawkers were her only friends when she was "a cross-eyed, ugly-duckling" child.

Hands Around the Lake culminated with a human chain that reached around the side of Prospect Park Lake.

As the crowd began to break up, Don found Marty and asked, "Did you like the speeches?"

"Letitia was the best. She tried to explain the magical healing power of nature," replied Marty.

"I wouldn't understand," said Don, who then asked, "Do you know who rounded up the geese?"

"Yes, it's a guy called Bill Bruford who works for the Department of Agriculture, the USDA, but he has a team of helpers," Marty replied.

"Wasn't he the drummer for King Crimson and Yes?"

"You're not the first person to notice the name, but it's not the same guy." Then Marty said, "Do you want to see something?"

"Sure, but why are you not miserable today like everyone else?"

"I'm an optimist."

"You have something up your sleeve. You are up to something."

"Come with me."

Marty led Don around the lake towards East Drive and started the climb towards Grand Army Plaza.

"Where are we going?" Don asked.

"You will see. We are going by Nellie's Lawn and the Battle Pass," Marty replied.

Marty slowed on the hill and Don slowed down with him, "We have to leave the road. Over here," Marty continued.

Over here was to the right side of the roadway and into a wooded area just beyond a semi-circular grassy area. To get there, they had to cross the bike lane and compete for space with cyclists, runners, and a girl on roller skates. Once past the bike lane, they walked on the grass at the side of the road.

"Where are you taking me?" Don asked.

"Slow down, my legs aren't what they used to be," Marty replied.

"Take a rest. There's a great view of the Long Meadow from here."

But Marty continued slowly onto a path and passed a sign identifying the area as the Vale of Cashmere. There was also an elaborate dirt-bike track with ramps made from piles of earth that wound its way through the trees. The path Marty followed was marked but overgrown, and Marty stopped frequently to push aside overhanging branches.

"This had better be good," Don said.

"To the north of here there were several abandoned ponds that have dried up and are filled with weeds," Marty said.

"And?"

Marty said nothing, but he did turn and smile mischievously. He then turned off the dirt path and down a slope to a rocky hollow.

Don followed, looking around, and said, "There is nothing here."

Marty moved some small oak branches away and uncovered his chicken coop. Then, crouching down to look inside the coop, said "Look in here. Come meet Pink, Puff, and Pickle."

Don looked and exclaimed, "You have goslings! They're adorable. Look at those fat bodies and scrawny necks. What's the noise? And when you have six of them, why do only three of them have names?"

"I keep a tape recorder going with a recording of goose sounds. It exercises the goslings' brains. I firmly believe that babies should be read stories and be sung to."

"Which one is Pink and which one is Puff?"

"Pink is the one at the front, he would not leave me when I had him at home. Puff might be the only female."

"What's that at the back of the coop?"

"It's a little diorama that I made. They used to huddle up to it when I first brought them here, probably because they were cold. The background is a painting of Prospect Park Lake. It's a water scene and there's a real water pool in front of the background. I have some spinach that I'm going to drop in the water for their lunch."

"Is that what you feed them?"

"Spinach today, but also I collect weeds, and I have a bag of corn. The weeds they like best are the little ones with the yellow flowers."

"Dandelions."

"No, they will eat dandelions. but they prefer groundsel. The groundsel has a bitter taste."

"You have to go looking for weeds?"

"Yes, you can't buy weeds. I sometimes go up by the abandoned ponds and fill a bag."

"Does Tanisha know about this?"

"No, but I did ask her, you know, about the legal aspects. "

"What did she say?"

"She laughed."

"Did you bring the goslings here from the Prospect Park Lake?"

"No, I bought them online from Stromberg's Chickens. They are wild goslings, Canadian honkers. They came in the mail in a ventilated cardboard box, they were tiny when they got here and I kept them in my apartment for a month. They have grown a lot since I moved them to the park. I was worried in case the mail was delayed, but I have a neighbor who keeps chickens in his backyard, and he has never had a problem ordering chicks by mail."

"What did you pay for them?"

"Thirty-one dollars and ninety-five cents each. The minimum order was six, and shipping was free."

"What do you plan to do with them?"

"I think we need a plan B, in case we can't save the few geese that are left on the lake. I'm going to keep them here until they are two months old, and then I'm going to walk them down to the Prospect Park Lake."

"You think that they will follow you?"

"I've been training them. They identify with me. They think I'm their father."

"Won't they fly away?"

"They won't fly until they are two-and-a-half months old."

"You do know that they are mostly males?"

"How do you know?"

"Their color and their body language."

"I bought straight run goslings, they were cheaper."

"But they won't breed."

"Probably not, and possibly they won't stay in the park after they learn to fly. But, no matter, even if they only stay a few weeks, the sight of goslings by the lake will piss off the Prospect Park Alliance and the United States Department of Wildlife Services, the bastards who killed the geese."

Night Patrol in Prospect Park

Marty and Tanisha met up at the Park Circle at the southwest corner of the park at two a.m. They had flashlights, a flask of coffee, cell phones, a megaphone, air horns, rattles, and noise-makers. They planned to use the cell phone to send a group alert to Goose Watch if they needed help. The rattles and noise-makers were to scare off Wildlife Services, who liked to operate in secrecy.

"Why are we here?" asked Marty, "I thought that you were saving the geese at the airport."

"The geese here are considered to be a threat to the airport. They are rounding up geese within a seven-mile zone," Tanisha replied.

"But why tonight?"

"The United States Department of Wildlife Services was seen here last night, they hammered in some survey stakes by the pond."

Tanisha was wearing a dark hoodie and carrying a water bottle from the Goose Feather Café. The water bottle had an "I've got goose" label on it.

"I put my name down on the volunteer list and they called me," Tanisha continued.

"Happens," Marty replied.

They fell into silence until they entered the park, "Clockwise?" Marty asked.

"Clockwise?" Tanisha questioned.

"Should we go clockwise around the park?"

"Okay."

"Turn left," said Marty, and they started to follow the road together, going clockwise around the lake.

"Is this the first time that you have been here at night?" asked Marty.

"Yes," Tanisha replied.

It was a warm night, and the road inside the park was well lit and empty. On Prospect Park South West, which circled the outside of the park, Marty could see the car traffic. Looking into the park, he could see the outline of the lake, but it was too dark to see if there were any geese on it.

As they turned to follow the north side of the lake, Tanisha said, "It does not look anything like this during daytime."

"What's different?"

"Watch the shadows of the trees from the street lights. Watch the shadows move with the wind."

"Are you scared?"

"A bit, but it seems safe enough. Let's move on."

The road turned away from the lake, and Marty turned off the road and onto a path that followed the lake. There were no lights along the path, but there was enough light for him to see ahead without turning on his flashlight. The path led them around wire fences that were protecting newly planted trees. They had to step over or walk around trees downed by high winds. When they stepped off the path, there were brambles, thorns, and what Marty thought was poison ivy. Marty stopped to listen for any sign of Wildlife Services activity.

"There's a better path over there," Tanisha said.

"Keep quiet, I want to listen," Marty replied.

"Listen for what?"

"It's never totally dark, so you can't spot the lights used by Wildlife Services. I need to listen for the noise from the truck, listen for the diesel engine."

"There's nothing out there"

"Be quiet, let's not talk for 10 minutes. Get used to the quiet and listen carefully for engine noise."

After the 10 minutes had elapsed, Marty checked his watch. It was five a.m. As far as he could tell, they were the only people in the park.

After another 10 minutes, Marty asked, "Do you hear it?"

"No," Tanisha replied.

"There's a rumble from a diesel truck. Let's go down to the lake. We'll be able to see when we get out of the trees."

Tanisha went ahead, carefully making her way through the bushes.

At the lake edge, Tanisha stopped, "You are right. There is a truck and four guys on the other side of the lake. They are near the new survey stakes," she said as she turned towards Marty.

"Can you tell what they are doing?

"They are bent over. They might be oiling eggs."

"And?"

"They spray the eggs with oil to block the pores and prevent goslings from hatching. Or, they addle the eggs by shaking them until the embryo collapses; this way, the goose will stay nesting but the chick won't hatch. From the photo that you showed me, I think the guy with the flashlight could be Bruford. The small guy with him is probably Donny. The other big guy, standing a little away from them, might be the biologist. It's hard to tell in this light."

"What do we do?"

"I don't know, most of the geese were rounded up and gassed. I guess that they came back to take care of the eggs."

"Let's make a racket. These guys don't like attention. Give me the megaphone and you take the rattle. We'll make noise for two minutes and then retreat before they have a chance to get over here."

Marty took the megaphone and with it set to the highest volume, said "Egg oilers. Give yourself up. Put your hands on your heads. Drop your oil cans. We know who you are. Resistance is futile."

Tanisha swung the rattle around her head.

Bruford killed his flashlight.

Marty repeated his "egg oilers" message two more times before saying to Tanisha, "Let's get out of here."

"Shouldn't we send a group alert?" Tanisha asked.

"Yes, but when we are clear of the lake," Marty replied.

There were noises as they left, but not the noise of diesel engines. There were city noises in the distance, insect and unidentified bird noises nearby, and after they traveled about a quarter of a mile, they distinctly heard a man's voice. It, however, didn't sound like the voice of a wildlife service employee. It sounded like a homeless man, talking to himself, giving himself instructions on how to prosper. How to lead a good life, and how everything in the world would be all right if everyone feared God. Marty had wondered why homeless people choose to live in the Park and had concluded that it was because they valued their privacy, as there was no privacy if you lived on a street corner in Manhattan. Marty and Tanisha respected the homeless man's privacy and altered course to go around him.

They walked another quarter of a mile in silence before Tanisha said, "Let's take a rest and send the group alert."

And they sat down on a bench near the drummer's circle and Marty offered Tanisha black coffee, which they drank from the same cup. They knew little about each other but they were now friends, and they were looking out for each other. Marty and Tanisha had developed a trust, like Boy Scouts who had camped out together in the woods. They had become close.

Dawn was breaking. The sky was starting to lighten in the east, and they now had a view of the lake. Moving down to it, they saw seven geese and two American black ducks on the water. A year back, before the roundups, there were hundreds of geese and mallards on the lake. Marty thought about the two American black ducks; their color had saved them. It was likely that Bruford and his crew had not been able to see the black ducks when they rounded up the birds at night. The bright green-and-white plumage of the male mallards had sealed their fate.

Tanisha seemed to know what Marty was thinking and said, "It's a good thing that the American black ducks didn't breed with the mallards. Interbreeding between mallards and black ducks would have resulted in light-skinned ducklings, and that would have sealed the ducklings' fate."

Walking the Goslings to the Lake

Three geese in a flock
one flew east
one flew west
one flew over the cuckoo's nest
    —Children's counting-rhyme quoted by Ken Kesey in One Flew Over the Cuck-
oo's Nest

Marty chose the last Sunday in May to walk the goslings down to the lake. The park would be busy on a weekend, and he might get some support on the way. He planned to pick the goslings up from the chicken coop at the Vale of Cashmere and take them to the Well House on Wellhouse Drive. He'd brought a cardboard box from his apartment to carry the goslings to the Well House. From there, he planned to take the goslings out of the box and walk them to the lake.

Marty met Tanisha and Don met by Grand Army Plaza. When they met, Don surprised everyone. He was wearing a smart, two-piece suit, a red tie, and a Goose Watch badge. His suit was gray and just a little darker than his salt-and-pepper beard.

"Why the suit?" asked Marty.

"I can get away with a lot when I'm wearing a suit," replied Don as he laughed self-consciously.

Taking his eyes off Don, Marty saw that Tanisha was wearing a bright red windbreaker and jeans. The wind was blowing her hair around.

Marty's dress was nondescript, showing not much shape and full pockets. He wasn't going to get away with anything.

"What's the plan?" Tanisha asked as Marty gestured that they should enter the park.

"We're going to pick up the goslings from the Vale of Cashmere, put them in the cardboard box, and carry them down to the lake," replied Marty.

"How much have they grown?" asked Don.

"They've been growing like crazy. They will soon be able to fly."

As they entered the Vale of Cashmere, Tanisha said, "I've never been to this part of the park before."

"It's named after a valley in Kashmir, it's been neglected for years, nobody much comes here," replied Marty.

"So that's why you're keeping the goslings here," said Tanisha.

"Yes," Marty replied.

Tanisha then pointed to the side of the path, "I never saw a tree like that. I love the tubular white flowers."

"It's a shrub, bottlebrush buckeye. I saw it a couple of weeks back and I looked it up. Notice the pink stems," said Marty.

"Where are the goslings?" asked Tanisha.

"Nearby. We have to leave the paved path and follow a dirt path to the chicken coop that I'm keeping the goslings in. I've covered the chicken coop with branches to hide it," replied Marty.

They couldn't even see the entrance to the dirt path, as an overhanging branch hid it. They pulled it to the side, but there were more overhanging branches as they continued. Marty then descended into a hollow, just off the path, and started to pull to the side the oak tree branches that he'd used to cover the coop. He then lifted the lid off the coop and looked inside.

"Let me see," said Tanisha.

"They have come to identify with me. I think I've imprinted them with my voice and my smell," said Marty.

"I wish I'd visited the goslings when they were chicks," said Tanisha.

"They were really fluffy and soft when they were chicks. Now they are growing flight feathers," replied Marty.

"They are still cute. Do any of them have names?"

"I named three of them. There's Pink, Puff, and Pickle. Pink has a pink patch on his right side. Puff's feathers puff up a lot, and Pickle seemed always to be lost—in a pickle."

Marty picked up a gosling from the coop and held it up for Tanisha to see, "This one is Pink. It's got a pink patch, and also I tied a small piece of pink wool to its leg." And then after pausing to put Pink back in the coop he continued, "We'll leave the chicken coop, the painting, and the water pool here. I will come back and pick them up later."

One by one, Marty and Tanisha moved the goslings from the chicken coop to the cardboard box.

"Which way out?" asked Tanisha.

"There is only one way out. We have to go back the way that we came," Marty replied.

Once on the dirt path, they walked in single file, Marty leading the way followed by Tanisha and Don. Marty was carrying the cardboard box with the goslings.

As they crossed a dirt-bike path, Tanisha asked, "Do the bikers bother you?"

"No. I don't bother them and they don't bother me. Neither of us is supposed to be here," Marty replied.

The dirt path led to the wider, red-brick path where the red bricks were set into the dirt.

Here, Tanisha caught up with Marty and said, "The Vale of Cashmere is like a park within a park. It's completely different from the rest of Prospect Park."

As they left the shelter of the Vale of Cashmere, the sun shone through the trees, and the wind found its way into the thinning tree cover, creating moving shadows of tree leaves.

Emerging on to East Side Drive, Don caught up with Tanisha and Marty, and there was room for them to walk three abreast. They continued to walk this way for the rest of the journey.

"It looks like you are starting to like geese," said Tanisha, flashing Marty a big smile.

"I've become fond of the goslings. I kept them at home for a month, and I've visited them every day since I moved them to the park. I had to sleep with my hand in their box the night they arrived in the mail. Otherwise, they would not stop cheeping," said Marty.

"Will they be okay on the lake?" asked Don, who, for once, looked concerned.

"If they were wild, they would still be with their parents," replied Tanisha.

"Will they be okay?" asked Don again.

"Their only enemies in the park are dogs and maybe red-tailed hawks," replied Tanisha.

"And it's unlikely that there will be another goose roundup after the Hands Around the Lake protest," said Marty.

"And visitors from Park Slope will feed them non-GMO, organic corn," said Don.

After crossing the busy East Drive, crammed with cyclists and runners, Marty was starting to enjoy himself. Payback was sweat. From Wellhouse Drive, they had a view of the lake, their eventual destination. Then the road climbed and the lake was no longer visible, but at the top of the hill, you could see it again, and Marty also caught a view of the Well House. Here, Marty felt the need for a rest, so he put the cardboard box down. As he sat down, a couple approached from the opposite direction, and two goslings poked their heads out of the box to greet them.

"Where did you get them?" asked the man.

"I raised them from chicks," Replied Marty, as the couple moved close to the box.

"Where are you taking them?" asked the man.

"To the lake by the Well House," replied Marty.

"Why?"

"We're replacing the geese that were rounded up and killed last summer."

"We read about the killings in the *Brooklyn Paper*."

"We only have a few replacements."

"Do you mind if we watch?" asked the woman.

"We'd welcome your support," replied Marty.

The couple looked to be in their fifties. What stood out about them, though, was their stout shoes and walking sticks. The woman was blond and wore green pants. The guy wore glasses and was bald. When they all started again, the couple led the way. Experienced hikers, they swung their sticks as they walked ahead of Marty.

"Can we carry the goslings all the way down to the lake?" asked Don as they got to the Well House.

"No, they are going to walk the next part. I've spent a lot of time imprinting myself on the goslings, and they will walk behind me. I don't want to waste the training. I want a picture of them walking. We'll take them out of the box here, and I'll lead them down to the lake," replied Marty.

"How do you know that they will follow you?" asked Don.

"I practiced walking with them in my apartment," replied Marty. "They have been with me since they were chicks. They slept next to me. They know my voice. They know my smell."

Marty and Tanisha picked up the goslings one by one from the box and put them in a row on the ground. Pink was first, as Pink always approached first whenever Marty put his hand in the box. The others followed. When he picked up Pickle, Marty attached the goose's harness and leash. Pickle had never willingly followed Marty; he would have to lead the goose to the lake.

Marty said, "Up-one-two, up-one-two, up-one-two, up-one-two," as he started off towards the lake.

The goslings followed, one after the other in a straight line, waddled to the lake. Pickle's waddle was unique, the steps were high, as Marty was lifting Pickle a little off the ground as he pulled him ahead.

Marty resisted the temptation to goose-step, as he wanted this to be a solemn moment, but he did notice that there was something about the goslings' goose-step that was assertive. It was as though the goslings were asserting their right of way. It was a proud moment for Marty.

Two children came over and one asked, "Can we pet them?"

"Not now," replied Marty. "I need them to concentrate on getting to the lake."

By this time, Don, in his suit, was managing a small crowd that had gathered on both sides of the path that the goslings would take from the Well House to the lake. Don smiled as he handed out Goose Watch badges and pointed to the badge on his jacket lapel. Tanisha pushed into the crowd to get a picture. As Marty and the goslings reached the lake, the small group of people who had been standing at the lakeside moved to let them through.

Stopping at the water's edge Marty was not sure what to do next. It was Tanisha who unclipped Pickle's harness and gently pushed Pickle into the water. Once in the water, Pickle splashed and swam with delight.

There was a round of cheers as Pickle swam away.

There were more cheers as the other goslings followed. Beating their wings and blowing through their bills, trying to fly as they swam away. They were natural swimmers once they got into the water.

Marty's plan to replace the geese on the lake, however, had a bitter-sweet ending. There were now a few geese, three American black ducks, and six goslings out on Prospect Park Lake. Before the goose roundup of last summer, there had been hundreds of American black ducks, hundreds of mallards, and more than 300 Canada geese.

Rikers Island Geese

Marty had to join a prison ministry to get to the geese at Rikers Island, and his trip to Rikers started with an early morning prayer service at a Manhattan Church, which was followed by a bus trip. At the prayer service, the congregation prayed for an old man, T. D. Levy, who had been a prisoner at Rikers for the past 15 years. Levy was well known to the congregation who, for the most part, seemed to think that he had been wrongly imprisoned.

The ministry's bus headed first to Queens and then over the bridge to Rikers Island. The ministry had five members, a priest and four helpers. On the bus the priest handed out Bibles, prayer books, and hymnal's. In addition to those books, Marty was also carrying his own copy of John Bunyan's *The Pilgrim's Progress*, a fictional account of theological beliefs and prison, which he planned to read on the way.

Getting out of the bus, Marty looked around; from the car-park he couldn't see the water, the beach, trees, grass, or any geese. It was a concrete-and-asphalt jail. Walls blocked his view on all sides.

Indoors in the security area, guards searched the ministry for drugs before the ministry passed through a metal detector. After the metal detector, the group picked up two prison guards who escorted them on the short walk to the Rose M. Singer Chapel. On the walk, Marty tried to hang back from the group and look over the wall that ran alongside the path. He gripped the top of the wall and pulled himself up.

"Mister Marty, you have to stay with the group," said the priest as he grabbed Marty's arm to pull Marty down.

Marty might have expected a guard to stop him, not the priest.

The Rose M. Singer Chapel was a single, windowless room with dull, gray cinder-block walls and one door. There was a central aisle and rows of wooden pews on each side. There was no piano or organ, and Marty realized that he wouldn't be using the hymnal. The air inside the chapel was stale, as there was no ventilation, there were also no flowers near the altar and no Bibles on the racks in the pews.

The prisoners arrived next, and the priest quickly hugged each prisoner as he entered. The third one was Levy; Marty realized this as the priest greeted Levy by name and a hug that could pass for a real hug. Levy seemed healthy enough for a long-term prisoner. His hair was short, and his face was bony. From his appearance, Marty guessed that he had not shaved for a couple of days.

After the sixth and last prisoner entered the chapel, a guard locked the door. And, as if to make sure that nobody got out, the two guards stood by it. The priest was at the front of the chapel. The prison ministry in the second row of pews, and the inmates two rows behind. Most of the chapel was empty.

The priest gave Marty a short prayer interceding for T. D. Levy to read; he had inserted it in the prayer book before he gave it to Marty. Marty was to read it when he got the nod.

"Let's pray," the priest said.

From his pew, Marty said, "Let's pray for T. D. Levy. In Jesus's name, please hear our prayers and release T. D. Levy from Rikers jail. May all the charges against him be dropped so that he does not spend his final years in jail. Thank you in Jesus's name."

When done, Marty turned and approached the chapel door.

"Where are you going?" asked the guard on his right, blocking Marty's path.

"I'm a visitor, I'm going to take a look around," replied Marty.

"You are not allowed outside the chapel," said the guard, "go back to your seat."

Marty felt defeat as he went back to his seat.

Marty's grandmother had been religious. She had no difficulty talking about her beliefs, and she put them out there whenever she could. Marty's parents had also been regular church-goers and, when he was a child at home, they said grace before each meal. Marty was much more private and, when he thought about it, an agnostic. He had no real investment in the church or the prison ministry. He did, however, care for people, and he'd got quite emotional when he had read the second sentence of the prayer for Levy.

Toward the end of the service, Marty realized that Levy did interest him. Was he really not guilty and wrongly imprisoned? The presence of the priest and the prison guards made access to Levy difficult. Marty stepped back two rows to be closer to him. Levy was listening to the service but seemed uninvolved. On his right wrist, he was wearing a dirty white braided rope bracelet that he looked to have made himself. Above the bracelet was a tattoo of an anchor.

Edging his way along the pew, Marty asked Levy, "How long is your sentence?"

The priest said, "Shush."

Unable to talk, Marty remembered his childhood in church and wrote his question out in a note, which he passed to Levy.

When he got the note back, Levy had written 'LIFE' over Marty's question.

"Why?" Marty questioned.

"I'm a USS *Leopold* survivor," penned Levy.

Marty realized that Levy must be at least 80 years old.

Then Levy spoke, ignoring the priest's shushing, saying, "I lost most of my mates. There's been a ringing in my ear since that ship blew up. I should have gone down with the ship."

Marty also ignored the shush and said, "I'm sorry."

On the way out back to the bus, Marty again tried to look over the wall. This time he was quicker pulling himself up the wall and looking over. There was a path on the other side of the wall that led to the water and maybe the geese, but he couldn't see much.

Again the priest pulled him down, "Mister Marty, we have to stay with the group," said the priest.

Marty knew that Rikers Island had a long history of geese roundups. The roundups started six years ago and were still going on. Each summer, crews killed approximately 300 geese on the island. The department of corrections had (according to freedom of information requests that Marty had read) given the United States Department of Agriculture

Wildlife Services, the USDA, access to the geese on the island and placed no restrictions on the number of geese that could be killed. The geese on the island weren't behind bars like T.D. Levy was, but most of them were on death row. There was nothing that Marty could do about this.

The Jamaica Bay Wildlife Refuge

In a rare splurge of funds, Marty rented a car so that he and Tanisha could view the geese at the Jamaica Bay Wildlife Refuge. The last part of the car trip was south, down Cross Bay Boulevard. They were not to cross the toll bridge to the Rockaways, but exit to the right, into the wildlife refuge car park. As they got close, Marty heard a plane taking off and watched the low-flying plane turn south. They were close to Kennedy.

With the airplane so close, Marty asked, "Why didn't they round up the geese here before the roundup at Prospect Park?"

Tanisha pointed at the plane and then at her ears, "I can't hear you above the noise," she shouted.

Marty waited a bit for the noise to die down, "We are really close to the airport. Why did they take their time rounding up geese here?" he asked.

"It's a wildlife refuge. The park service won't give them permission."

"But won't there be pressure?"

"The park service manages the wildlife refuge. I think that there is pressure from the airport and the United States Department of Wildlife Services, the USDA."

"Is that all?"

"No, New York Senator Kirsten Gillibrand is pushing for it. She has a bill to allow the USDA to "remove" Canada geese from here in June and July when they are molting and can't fly."

"She should have stuck to her job with Philip Morris as a defender of big tobacco and not moved into politics. She should have stuck with killing people, not moved on to killing geese."

It was a breezy and warm July day. Tanisha was wearing orange shorts and a pink t-shirt, but Marty was still dressed for cooler weather. As he got out of the car, he felt overdressed; he had not adjusted his wardrobe to the change in the season.

Once inside the visitor center, Marty looked around. This was his first visit to the wildlife refuge, and he was curious. He was looking at a poster for a kid's trip to collect bugs when a female park ranger approached him.

"Did you bring a small clear jar?" she asked.

"No," Marty replied.

"I'll get you one," she said.

Marty took the jar, "What's it for?"

"Aren't you going on the bug collection trip?"

"I don't think so."

And then she said, "I think we can collect a hissing cockroach."

Marty wasn't sure if she said kissing or hissing, but decided not to ask. It had been a while since he cleaned out the wax from his ears and hadn't expected either word. But he did have a few cockroaches at home, so he shook his head and smiled.

"Please?" she asked.

"I'll pass this time," Marty said.

Marty bought a souvenir bookmark and a bottle of water.

Seeing Marty turn to look at a map of the wildlife refuge, Tanisha said, "Let's go. I know the way."

"I'm looking at the map to see which way I can manage. The park ranger can probably help. I'm not as young as you," Marty replied.

"Which way is the West Pond?" Marty asked the park ranger.

"The trail starts out of the door and to the right. You can take the long trail or the short trail. The short trail is half a mile and the long trail one and a half miles."

"Can I take the map?" Marty asked.

"Yes. You also have to sign the visitor agreement."

Marty signed the visitor agreement and received a visitor's pass. There were rules printed on the back of the visitor pass. The rules seemed reasonable enough. One of them prohibited the killing of wildlife and this seemed to prohibit the killing of geese.

Once outside the visitor center, Marty and Tanisha followed the path as it wound its way through a wooded area. After a bit, it straightened out as it followed the shore of the West Pond.

"The long trail is a hike; can you make it?" Tanisha said.

"I'll take my jacket off and leave it in the car," Marty replied. But he didn't. He took the jacket off but left it hanging over his shoulder.

Marty started off down the trail heading north for a while, past a table with a log of recent bird sightings, and then turned to face a giant nest-box for birds that was on a 10-foot pole in the grass off the trail. The entrance was a circular six-inch hole, big enough for a parrot. Marty tried to look in the birdhouse, but even after craning his head he could not see inside. He threw a pebble at the nest box. Nothing flew out. It was empty.

"My impression is that there is little or no wildlife here," Marty said.

Further down the trail past the large nest-box, smaller nest-boxes showed up at regular intervals. Each was about five feet off the ground and nailed to a post. Marty peered into the first one. This was also empty except for some twigs left over from a previous occupant.

When they got to the fourth nest-box, Marty heard voices coming from the ocean side of the path, and he decided to investigate. There was a sign, "Protected area. Stay on the path" but there did not appear to be anything that needed protecting. He saw proof of that as he entered the bushes and saw the trash, the washed-up driftwood, and a washed-up 40-foot shipping container. The shipping container was red and its label said it was full of wood. It had a year on it, 1999, and the numbers 209174 22G1. The washed-up container was now someone's home. In front of the container, there were hot ashes from a driftwood campfire. Someone had left behind an empty bean tin, an empty tin of beef franks, a torn windbreaker, some charcoal lighter fluid, and a box of matches. Marty left quietly and went back to join Tanisha, who had not left the trail.

"What did you see?" Tanisha asked.

"There's the remains of a campfire. It looks like someone is camping out," Marty replied.

"There was also a homeless guy living in Prospect Park," Tanisha said.

They walked several hundred yards farther, past nest-boxes five and six, until Marty saw the small beach ahead at the side of West Pond. Approaching the beach, he had a clear view of the pond. It was the home to several hundred Canada geese and a similar number of mallards and American black ducks. The geese were mostly in the water, but the ones on the beach did not move as Marty approached.

"Can I take a closer look?" Marty asked.

"They don't seem to be afraid. You can go closer." Tanisha replied.

Marty stepped forward until he was a couple of feet from the geese, and then he bent down.

"You are too close, step back," Tanisha said.

"The goslings are bigger than the ones I took to Prospect Park," Marty replied.

"Get back!" Tanisha said.

"They are so cute," Marty said.

The two geese nearest to Marty bent their heads back slightly and then started to pump their heads up and down. It was sort of comical as they wobbled and pumped, but then the nearest goose started to honk and advance. Marty turned to walk away. The goose pecked at his heels.

"Face the goose and walk back slowly. Walk backwards," Tanisha said.

But it was too late. Marty was already running, with the gander in hot pursuit. Tanisha put herself in the path of the goose and turned to face it. The goose stopped.

A little shaken but unhurt, Marty asked, "What did I do?"

"You went too close. They are territorial and they will protect their young. The goslings stay with their parents until they are almost full grown. They are a bit like humans. They post guards. They look after their injured. They mate for life. Geese might look docile, but they can be vicious when they are protecting their young."

Marty sat on the ground near the road while the goose that had chased him retreated. Surprisingly, Marty was starting to like geese. He'd fallen in love with the goslings that he raised and was beginning to appreciate the way that geese protected their young.

"Is there anything that we can do to keep these geese safe?" Mary asked.

"I didn't know that you cared that much," Tanisha replied.

"I didn't use to," Marty said.

Tanisha confirmed Marty's fears "These geese might be beyond help. The Jamaica Bay Wildlife Refuge is next to the airport."

"Is that why Senator Gillibrand is trying to remove them?" Marty asked.

"Yes, the park service ought to protect the birds. Without waterfowl, the wildlife refuge will have to rely on bug-collection trips to attract visitors, and it will be hard for them to get New York City residents to come and collect hissing cockroaches," Tanisha replied.

After a bit, Marty started to walk back slowly and Tanisha followed. He read the sign about native plants. The prickly pear has a swollen stem and no leaves. The yucca has a long taproot. The common mullein has a thick layer of hair. They had all adapted to live on the small amount of water that's in the sandy soil of the marsh. Marty did recognize a few yuccas that were not flowering, but could not see any prickly pears or mullein. But maybe the sign was old and wrong. It didn't look as if anything much had happened here since the shipping container had washed up in 1999. The plant life was the usual South Brooklyn mix of brush, marsh grass, common reeds, and weeds. Marty was happy with this.

Before leaving the wildlife refuge, Marty took a last look northwest. Through the gaps in the plants, the bay was visible and it shone in the sunlight. Marty admired the view of the bay with Manhattan in the far distance.

Painting Marty's Boat

In June 2011, Marty called Tanisha to let her know that he was taking his boat out of the water so that he could paint the bottom before he took it out to Kennedy Airport again. He asked her if she would help, reminding her that she owed him a favor in return for having taken her out to the airport.

They met on a Saturday at two A.M. at the boatyard. Marty was planning to paint his boat while Tanisha acted as a lookout. Predictably, the owners had padlocked the gate to the boatyard, and when Marty suggested that she stay outside the yard and text him if anyone approached, she replied, "I'd feel safer on your side of the gate."

"Okay," said Marty.

Marty showed Tanisha the route that took them onto the beach and around the gate and left Tanisha hidden and to the side of the gate.

Marty then went inland and towards the back of the yard, lit a work light, and with a brush and a roller began to paint.

He'd painted almost half a side of the boat when his phone rang. "I'm cold. Do you have a Jacket?" Tanisha texted.

"Yes," Marty replied.

"Can you bring it to me? It's dark," Tanisha asked.

"Yes," Marty replied.

Pulling an old boating jacket from the cabin of his boat, Marty took it over. "Why do you have to do this at night?" she asked after she put the jacket on.

"The boatyard won't let you paint your own boat. They charge a lot of money for boat painting, and I don't have it."

"So, everybody sneaks in after midnight?"

"No, only me. The others don't have the gumption."

"You're unique."

"Stay here as lookout. I don't want to be caught."

Tanisha replied, "Okay."

And Marty headed back towards his boat.

An hour later, Marty finished the first coat of blue paint. He put down his brush, closed the paint can, put the work light out, and then went to check on Tanisha.

"There are animals out there," she said, pointing into the yard.

"What?" Marty asked.

"I saw eyes. I was being watched."

"It could have been a chicken or a rabbit or a cat."

"There are chickens here?"

"There are two. I feed them sometimes, and I collect their eggs when I find them. You can tell if you see chickens because chickens' eyes don't move. Chickens keep their eyes still by moving their heads to compensate for their wobbly legs. Rabbits jump and their eyes move with them. You can see them all over the place. There are more rabbits than chickens, we are near to Coney Island. At Coney Island, they do magic tricks and pull rabbits out of hats."

"Are you finished painting?"

"I have to do another coat. I will be finished in an hour. Stay on lookout for another hour and then come over."

Marty sat on the ground drinking tea from a thermos flask when Tanisha arrived.

"Can I have some?" she asked.

Marty poured some into the thermos flask cup-lid, "Be careful, it's hot," he said as he handed it over.

Marty sat still and looked around. Nothing moved except a warm breeze that carried the scent of grass. Looking up, Marty noticed that it was too bright to see stars. Lights from the bay masked the sky.

"You've done a good paint job. But I don't see why they won't let you paint your own boat." Tanisha said, looking at the boat.

"They say that the paint is toxic and has to be applied by a trained operator," Marty replied.

"Couldn't they show you?"

"It's a scam. It's about money. They have trained a Mexican. They wanted to charge me $250 to paint the boat. They pocket this and then pay a Mexican $30 to do the job. They also do a lousy job. They don't wash off the dirt before they paint, and the paint falls off."

"What's the training?"

"It's to prevent paint spills."

"Does it work?"

"Not if you pay minimum wage."

"But won't they notice the fresh paint on your boat?"

"There is a good chance that they will. I would not be surprised if they accuse the Mexican of painting the wrong boat."

"Won't he deny it?"

"He does not speak English."

"You should throw some dirt on the fresh paint. The dirt will wash off when the boat goes into the water. I don't want you to get the Mexican in trouble."

When Marty didn't answer but threw dirt on the freshly painted boat, Tanisha asked, "Can we go home?"

"Yes, let me put away the paint and the work light," Marty replied as he smiled.

"Are you sure that you needed a lookout? Nobody comes back here," Tanisha said.

"The sooner we get this done, the sooner we can rescue geese. I needed your help. I will get thrown out of the marina if I am caught," Marty replied.

"Why?"

"The Department of Environmental Conservation monitors boat painting. They check the chemical makeup of boat paints for toxins, and they check how the paints are applied. They fine the marina for violations. There are large fines."

"You do know that I'm a law student, and that you are breaking the law?"

"Yes, I do. My advice is that you keep quiet about it."

"Why?"

"You are an accomplice."

Tanisha looked out into space as though she was thinking about what to do. She then looked down.

"When will you be ready to go out to Kennedy Airport if we have to rescue geese?" she asked.

"I have to launch the boat first. The weekend would be best for going out to Kennedy. There will a lot of boats out on the water on the weekend, and there is less chance of being noticed. Don't wear orange or red when we go out to the airport, or you will be seen," Marty replied.

"Is there anything else I need to know?"

"No. Let's go. We're done."

"Not quite. Your face is blue. You need to wash the paint off your face."

PART THREE

138.   DEAD HORSE BAY

The Wild Goose Chase

Look, we try to start very early in the morning so that the geese don't overheat. When they are in our care, we have to take the best possible care of them.
—Lee Humberg, Biologist, New York Magazine, Summer 2011.

Marty was surprised when he got a warning of a goose roundup at Kennedy. He received a phone call from Tanisha, who had heard from her husband, who worked at the airport as an airport security guard. Tanisha's husband had told her that the roundup was to take place the next day.

"Why doesn't Don travel with us?" asked Tanisha, as she got into Marty's boat.

"Don won't travel with me anymore. He didn't feel safe the last time we came out here," replied Marty.

"Why?"

"The boat heeled, and Don is heavy."

"Where is he?"

"He's borrowed an inflatable; he plans to join us later."

Tanisha and Marty left Dead Horse Bay early—three A.M. The plan was to get to the airport by six A.M., soon after it got light but before the geese roundup started.

On the boat, Marty took out a paper chart of Jamaica Bay and studied it using the small red light that he used for night vision. He planned to steer to the lighted buoys using the compass course direction that he had marked on the chart. In the meantime, Tanisha was checking the GPS and the weather on her phone and appeared to Marty to be somewhat amused by Marty and his chart. In the dark, Marty couldn't see her facial expression clearly, but he was happy to have her company.

Leaving the marina was uneventful, as rows of lights at close intervals illuminated the docks, and they could distinctly see the gap in the breakwater. In open water outside the breakwater, two bands of light bounded the bay. To the north, there were the headlights of cars on the Belt Parkway, and to the south, there were lights from a few of the houses in the Rockaways. In the center, and very faint, were the red and green lights of navigation buoys numbers nine and ten, and this was where Marty was heading.

The next buoy, buoy 20, was over by the Rockaways. It had a red light that flashed every six seconds. Marty watched until it flashed and then waited six seconds to see if it flashed again. When it did, he turned the boat towards it.

"Can't we go faster? The GPS shows our speed as three knots," Tanisha said.

"The engine is old, I can't run it at full throttle," Marty replied.

"So then, why do we have to go the long way around?" asked Tanisha, again looking at the GPS.

"I told you the last time that we came out here. We can't skip the dogleg or we'll run aground," Marty replied.

Marty then followed the deep-water channel that led inland under the Gil Hodges Memorial Bridge and towards the airport. Channel buoys marked either side of the channel. There were also lights on the bridge towers. Marty had to steer a straight line from light to light.

Just past the bridge, Marty rubbed his shoulder as a reflex, remembering the jibing accident that occurred on his first trip out here with Tanisha. Then he felt the current pulling the boat along and decided to let the boat drift for a while. It was quiet and peaceful on Beach Channel. Marty gave Tanisha the tiller and then started to doze. He was surprised at how much he now trusted her. He hadn't trusted her at first because she'd contradicted herself when she said that she never saw her husband, but this was the third time that they had been out to Kennedy Airport, and she had never let him down.

Marty woke suddenly to find Tanisha jabbing his ribs.

"What's that coming towards us?" she asked.

"A tugboat," Marty replied.

"In the middle of the night?" Tanisha said.

"It should keep to the right."

"There is something behind it."

"It is towing a barge."

As the tugboat got closer, Marty could see its deck and navigation lights—two masthead lights, one above the other, Marty knew that this meant that it had a tow. The tug's cabin was a dirty brown color with a white ring on the funnel. The letter M was visible underneath the white ring, probably the initial of the company that owned the tug. The crew was inside, but the tug was in the channel and moving fast. The barge itself was black and larger than the tug, and Marty could see what looked like fuel hoses. It was probably a fuel barge heading for the East River.

"I'm glad that you knew that it was towing a barge. I didn't know," Tanisha said.

"The tug might be on autopilot. But hold on tight, it's going to pass close and its wake is going to hit us," Marty replied.

Marty took the tiller and turned his boat so it crossed the tug's wake at a right angle. Looking ahead, he could see the white ripples and hear the water's movement.

When the bobbing from the tug's wake died down, Marty loosened his grip on the coaming and turned to Tanisha. She was still holding on. Marty told her that they had crossed the wake and that she could relax and let go.

"I was scared," Tanisha said.

As they left Beach Channel, Marty saw her switch between the GPS on her phone and a weather app until she lost phone service when they went under the second bridge.

"Can you find the way from here?" She asked Marty.

"I know the area. It will be light before we get to the airport." Marty replied.

By five A.M., it was light and the sun was coming up. It was still cool, but from the strength of the sun, Marty could tell that it was going to be a hot day. The sun lit up the airport and the channel that led to it and Grassy Bay.

Marty looked at Tanisha, she had just a touch of a smile and was wide-eyed as she put on sunglasses and turned to look at the airport. Marty's black-and-white picture of Tanisha turned to color. She was wearing a purple sports bra and red leggings with a cat motif. Tanisha had binoculars and a camera hanging from her neck. Her hair stood up as though it had just been picked. For a moment, her hair blocked Marty's view as it sparkled and shone in the sun.

Turning back towards Marty, Tanisha said, "You look more like a mariner than an eco-defender. Look at your open-neck shirt and your sunburnt neck, and the rope armband around your wrist. It's a shame about your skinny arms and knees. Most mariners are built." and at that, she began to laugh.

Marty agreed with her, but he didn't want to give her the satisfaction of knowing this.

Marty had a clear view of the airport. The beach looked narrow, but behind it there was marsh grass, scrub bushes, and some small trees. Then there was the airport fence, made of metal, maybe nine feet tall. There was a gate in the airport fence and a small road ran through it from the airport to the beach. A pile of poultry crates was stacked near the gate. Behind the airport fence, he made out fuel tanks, runways, hangers, and a control tower. They could see several airplanes in the distance, mostly passenger jets.

Marty tapped Tanisha's arm, asking, "Can I look through your binoculars?"

"You don't need them. There is nothing happening. Can you take the boat in closer and tie it up?" Tanisha replied.

"Okay," Marty replied.

He then started to move towards the shore. When the boat went aground on the sandy bottom, Marty took a rope onto the beach and tied it to a tree root. There was nobody around to notice their arrival.

"It feels good to be on land," Tanisha said.

A little way from the boat, she put down a blanket and sat down on it. When Marty sat down next to her, she caught him off guard when she took out granola bars and water from her backpack and handed them to him. She had up until now always taken his food, and this was the first time that she had given him something to eat.

Some 15 minutes later, Marty heard the noise of an engine and looking around, saw that a truck had driven up to the gate in the airport fence and that the driver was unlocking the gate to allow the truck onto the beach. Six guys, including Bruford's sidekick Donny, got out of the truck and began unloading kayaks, paddles, life vests, netting, and posts. They then carried these down the beach along with the poultry crates that had been stacked by the gate.

Donny began hammering in posts near the water, and another guy was stringing the netting between them to create a corral. The corral was square with a wide entrance that got narrower where it entered the square. Two other guys wore yellow vests and carried the kayaks. Just before they put the kayaks into the water, they donned life vests.

Soon after, three more guys turned up; they were talking in an animated way as they walked out to the beach from the airport gate. Marty turned to his left to focus on them. They were standing away from the group that had arrived in the truck. They were not setting up equipment, but they were talking a lot.

Marty pointed to this new group, "Who are they?" he asked.

"I think that they are supervising," Tanisha replied.

"Who is the guy in the suit?" Marty asked.

"He's the biologist. He must be Lee. The muscular guy is Bruford, and he is in charge. You can see that he has a walkie-talkie that he uses to give orders. The third guy looks like he works for the park service," Tanisha replied.

"Why is there a biologist?"

"He probably came up with the idea to catch the geese while they are molting. If it's Lee, he also claims to take care of the geese's comfort. For some reason, he doesn't want the geese to overheat."

"He's weird. He's devised a way to catch and kill the geese but he cares for their comfort?"

"There was an article about him in *New York Magazine*."

"The whole roundup is cruel. Why do they separate the adult geese from the goslings?" Marty asked.

"They don't gas the goslings. They squeeze their necks to dislocate the spine from the brain. The goslings die instantly," Tanisha replied.

Marty was both fascinated and horrified by the roundup, and it was a while before he could take his eyes off it. He had, in fact, not moved his head for 10 minutes and his mouth had stayed open this whole time. The two men in kayaks slowly cajoled the geese towards the shore. Once the geese were on land, the crew pushed the waddlers towards the corral entrance. From there, Donny, wearing long gloves, picked them up one at a time and put them into poultry crates that he then loaded onto the truck. The goslings, taken away from their parents, peeped loudly and constantly.

Tanisha shot a video of the roundup. Looking over her shoulder, Marty could see her camera's viewfinder as she zoomed in on the corral netting and then on Donny, who was still crating geese. The orange netting stood out in contrast to the bleached color of the beach. She then put the camera down and raised her binoculars.

"Can I see?" Marty asked, and then after a pause, "Where are they going to take the geese?"

"I don't know. They are secretive. They always black out locations on Freedom of Information Act responses. But they will take the geese away from the airport and gas them," Tanisha replied.

"Can we follow them?" Marty asked.

"We can't follow their truck through the airport, and even if we could, we couldn't keep up with them. They speed," Tanisha replied.

"So, we have to act now?"

"Yes."

Marty was feeling ill at ease. Even if Don did turn up, they were outnumbered and were likely to be arrested if they interfered. Marty had no idea what to do. He felt scared and nervous and helpless, and these were the three feelings he knew and recognized. He'd not felt so helpless since a girl he'd insulted in seventh grade had sat on him to prevent his escape while she called the teacher. He envied Tanisha's ability to calmly video the roundup.

"Can I have the binoculars?" Marty asked again, and this time Tanisha gave them to him.

Marty was perhaps 100 yards from the gate, and clearly, if either Bruford or Donny looked his way they would see him, but they were not looking. They were concentrating on the geese. Through the lenses, Marty stared at the poultry-transport crates that had been moved from the pile by the gate onto the beach. If he was right, these were the same crates that he had holed on his first visit to the airport. It was hard to be sure from where he was, the crates were stacked next to each other, and one crate's bars could hide other crate holes.

Marty handed the binoculars back, "I have to go in closer. I want to take a closer look at the crates," he said.

"I'm staying here," Tanisha replied.

Moving 50 yards closer, Marty cringed as he shouted a bright, "good morning" to Donny, who was creating a goose.

"Step back. This area is closed," Donny replied.

Marty stepped back a couple of steps. He tried to look confident but it was hard to look confident and step back. He'd probably be okay if he could do something, but what? Pull out the poles that were holding up the corral netting? Throw stuff at the geese so that they would run away? Run at the geese with his arms out to scare them?

Marty stepped forward, "What are you doing?" he asked.

"I told you to stay back. This area is closed," Donny replied.

But before he stepped back, Marty got a closer look at the poultry crates that Donny had filled with geese. At least two of the crates had holes. There was a hole visible in a crate at the end. Another crate had two holes, one at the front and the other at the back. They looked like the holes that he had made when they were out here at night, the cuts were uneven and there were sharp edges, and he remembered that he'd cut himself on one of them. He just wished that he had not stopped and had holed all the crates.

Marty was wondering how Donny could have missed this when Donny stepped towards him and again said, "step back."

Although Donny was a short guy, he had the advantage. He was heavyset and 40 years younger than Marty. Marty slowly walked back to the blanket where Tanisha was sitting.

"A few of the crates have holes in them," Marty said, Sitting down next to Tanisha.

"Don't you remember cutting the holes?" Tanisha replied.

"I cut holes in 40 or 50 crates, but I gave up after I cut my finger on a sharp piece of wire. They look to have replaced some of the crates that I holed," Marty said.

Tanisha began to smile, "Yes. But they missed some," she said.

Marty, taking the binoculars again said, "The goslings in the end crate could easily walk out."

"They are scared. They will stay put."

"The crates have holes. Why don't they bolt?"

"I could never figure out why free-range hens don't bolt. If I was a free-range hen, I would bolt the first time that I got the chance. I don't have mental hang-ups."

"We could tell Bruford that there are holes in his crates."

"Why?"

"He might not want to truck the geese to the poultry plant in crates that have holes. What if his truck goes around a corner and a goose falls out? If we tell him, he might start to repack the geese," Marty said.

"And?" Tanisha said.

"The more things he has to do, the more likely it is that he will make a mistake. Can you tell him?" Marty replied.

"Why me?" Tanisha asked.

"It's your turn to do something. Don't forget to smile as you talk."

Tanisha had to cross a soft area of sand and her leggings got a little wet on her way to tell Bruford. Closing in on Bruford, she was pulling the leggings up as she asked in a loud voice, "Are you in charge?"

Marty heard Tanisha but he could not hear Bruford's reply. It was probably a yes, as they were still talking.

Marty then heard Tanisha, who was talking loudly, say to Bruford, "There are holes in your crates."

Marty saw Bruford's lips move, but he again could not make out what he said. He did see the look on Bruford's face. Bruford did not look happy. Bruford then went over to where Donny was, put his hand into a holed crate, and said something to Donny. He then motioned for Lee Humberg to come over.

Tanisha returned, avoiding the soft sand.

"You told him?" Marty asked.

"You should have seen the look on his face," Tanisha replied.

"What did he say?" Marty asked.

"He said that the crates were new. He then told me to leave and then he went over to talk to Donny," Tanisha replied.

"Do we have to leave?"

"I'm not leaving. We have every right to be here. We are not on the airport. We are on the beach in Jamaica Bay."

"Did he say anything else?"

"No."

Tanisha put the binoculars to her eyes again.

"What do you see?" Marty asked.

Tanisha replied, "Bruford has gone back over to where Donny was stacking crates. They are trying to move the geese into new crates. They can't get the geese to leave the crates. Donny is poking one of the geese with a stick."

Tanisha put the binoculars down but then saw a movement and put them back to her eyes.

"One of the geese is out. It's scared. It's running off. It's naked. It has no feathers. Donny is chasing it. It's running towards the gate. It's going into the airport. It's going towards a runway," Tanisha said.

"Why don't they let that one goose go?" Marty asked.

"Aircraft ground crew are trying to head if off. It's a wild goose chase. Look at that goose move," Tanisha replied.

Marty heard a tiny thud and turned around to look. A gosling had fallen to the ground from a second holed crate. Two other goslings also fell, looked confused, and stood still for a minute. Then one of them started to walk along the beach. The others followed and when they arrived at a clump of weeds, they each took a bite before they split up. Marty, figuring that these goslings were too far away to be caught, tried to add to the confusion by pointing to them and yelled, "Over there!"

Marty's attempt to confuse failed, as Donny continued to chase the goose that was moving towards the runway. Yelling did help Marty, however, as he felt better now that he was doing something.

"Look at the goose. It's got to the runway. It's flapping its wings to take off but it can't fly. It's a little plump and wobbly and it can't run in a straight line. If it wasn't in danger, I would say that it looked cute," Tanisha said.

"I can imagine the control tower calling the goose. Come in goose one. Clear to take off goose one," Marty replied.

Tanisha looked puzzled, "The biologist is holding up his hand like he is signaling for them to stop chasing the goose," she said.

"Why does he want them to stop?" Marty asked.

"It's 90 degrees out here. The goose must be getting hot," Tanisha laughed.

"But why stop?"

"I keep forgetting that you didn't read the *New York Magazine* article about Lee Humberg. He is concerned for the geese's comfort. He has a thing about keeping them cool during the roundup. It does not make sense, but he wants the geese to be cool and calm when they are gassed."

Tanisha put the binoculars back to her eyes.

"Lee is talking to Bruford. They seem to be arguing. Now they are just glaring at each other," she said.

"What's going to happen next?" Marty asked.

Tanisha replied, "They are chasing the goose that's on the runway back towards the beach. Bruford is talking into the walkie-talkie. Donny is starting to release some of the geese. They might be giving up. Bruford has gone over to help Donny. They are both releasing geese. The corral netting is coming down. They are bringing the kayaks onto the beach. The roundup is over."

Don showed up too late to see the victory. As he approached in a small inflatable with an outboard, Don's single-barreled shotgun was visible to Marty, stowed across the seat. Don was wearing a Hawaiian shirt, pink shorts, and sunglasses. He kept flexing his arms as though he were showing off his muscles. He still looked like Don, however, his long black hair and a spotted salt-and-pepper beard gave him an overall scruffy look that he could not hide.

"How was the trip?" Marty shouted, as Don tilted the motor and pulled the inflatable onto the beach.

"I borrowed the inflatable but the motor kept stalling. When the engine stalled, I got carried backwards by the outgoing tide," Don replied.

"Why the Hawaiian shirt?" Marty asked.

"I don't want to be recognized near the airport. I'm scared of airport security," Don replied.

"Why?" Marty asked.

"Airport security got a little crazy after nine-eleven," Don replied.

"You would draw less attention to yourself if you put your shotgun away."

"Where?"

"Put it in the cabin of my boat."

"You do know that I'm a reformed duck hunter and that I don't shoot ducks anymore?"

"You still look like a duck hunter. And anyway, you missed all of the excitement," Marty said.

"What happened? It looks like they didn't take the geese," Don said.

"They started the roundup, but one goose escaped and they couldn't catch it," Marty replied.

"How did it escape?" Don asked.

"They put it into a crate that had a hole."

"But why did one escaped goose end the roundup?"

"They were chasing it and it got hot. Tanisha says that the biologist stopped the roundup because the goose was getting hot."

"And?"

"Lee Humberg, the biologist, likes to gas geese while they are cool and comfortable," Marty said.

"Has he a fetish?" Don asked.

Tanisha, who had been listening to the conversation broke in, "No. He just wants to kill them humanely."

"He's a barmpot. I use 600 milligram omega-three fish-oil tablets to cure brain fog and mood swings," Don replied.

"He will probably be back early tomorrow morning when it will be cool," Tanisha said.

And with that, Don walked off.

Looking at Marty, Tanisha said, "We did good today."

"I had a bad day. It was the worst thing, the feeling of helplessness that I felt during the roundup. I only started to feel better when I began to act. It felt good to be doing something, even if it didn't work," Marty replied.

At the same time, Marty realized just how little control he had over the situation, and just how valuable Betsey's advice was about studying the enemy.

"I wish I'd got video of the goose chase. It was funny," Tanisha said.

"You know, if Bruford had not decided to re-cage the geese, and if Lee was not concerned for the comfort of the geese, today would have ended differently," Marty replied.

The Nighttime Swim

"Geese actually sleep in the water, with a few geese taking shifts throughout the night to act as sentinels."
—Joan Morris, The Mercury News, September 2, 2015.

Marty knew that he had to be back at the airport early the next morning and so decided to stay out on the beach overnight. But after he was bit several times by mosquitoes, he decided to move off the beach. Taking Tanisha and Don with him, he got on his boat, pushed it out into the bay, and anchored away from the beach and the mosquitoes. It was peaceful at the anchor until Don, who had started to drink beer brought out a second can, put his head onto Marty's shoulder, and started to snore.

"Can you shoot straight when you are sober?" Marty asked as he pushed Don's head off his shoulder.

"I can shoot straight after I have had a beer," Don replied, and he went inside the boat to fetch his shotgun.

After loading and cocking the gun and drinking the remainder of his second beer, Don gave Marty the can and asked him to toss it into the air. It was getting dark, but when the can started to fall Don fired, plinking the can causing it to bounce in the air.

"Good shooting. I have a plan to save the geese and I might need your help," Marty said.

"Please put the gun away? It scares me," Tanisha said.

Don broke open the break-action shotgun and started to reply, but was interrupted by the noise of a jet taking off.

Marty looked up. The flashing lights on the jet's wings and the tail lit up the sky and behind these were the steady red and green lights on the wingtips. Marty felt the jet blast as the jet passed, and as it wasn't yet dark, the airplane cast a shadow on the water.

"I first heard a jet when I was in school in Canarsie. I was 10 years old and it was 1950. It must have been one of the first jets to take off from here and it flew over during assembly. It drowned out the headmaster. I was scared at first. I didn't know what it was," Marty said as the jet disappeared.

"Don, can you please put the shotgun away? I don't like guns," Tanisha shouted.

"It's a break-action gun, you can see that it's not loaded," replied Don.

"Pretty please, put it away."

This time Don put the gun away.

"You know, sometimes, Marty, I think that you only bring me out here because I know how to call ducks and geese. You don't ever pick my brain," said Don, when he returned from the boat's cabin.

"I don't?" Marty replied.

"Do you remember when we called the geese away from the airport?" Don asked.

"Yes, from Yellow Bar Hassock," Marty replied.

"You never asked what I thought of calling the geese away from the airport, or if I had a better plan."

"Did you? My plan worked until the geese flew off."

"Yes, we should have dug a tunnel. An escape route from the airport. We should have built a chute so that the geese could slide down it into the tunnel. You know that prisoners dug tunnels to escape from prison camps in World War Two—76 men escaped from Stalag Luft Three in 1944. Some of them were re-captured…" Don continued until a jet's noise drowned him out again. It was just minutes since the last jet had passed and this jet was lower. This time, it was darker and the jet made itself known solely by its noise and its lights. There was no shadow on the water anymore. Its power scared Marty.

"How would you have got the geese to go down your chute?" Marty asked.

"… There has to be a way. You can't expect me to think of everything," Don replied.

"Now that you are thinking about strategy, do you have a plan for tomorrow?" Marty asked.

"We could cut more holes in the crates," Don replied.

"We won't get away with that again. After today, they will check."

"You said that you had a plan."

"I have some ideas but nothing definite. We could call the geese over to the rocky area away from the airport fence gate. There is some cover there, and they would stand a better chance of escaping."

"Why?"

"They will have to carry their equipment over. They won't be able to bring their truck over. It will be more trouble for them. They might lose interest and give up."

"Is this your best plan?" Don asked.

"It's frustrating, the geese are protected by the migratory bird act, yet every request to kill geese gets the okay," said Tanisha.

Marty was, at first, glad when his phone rang, as it gave him a break from the conversation. He didn't have a plan for tomorrow, and he did not want Don to know. But as he realized that it was Betsey calling, he knew that he didn't want to talk to anyone except Tanisha and Don. Talking to someone outside this group would take his mind off saving geese.

"How are you?" Betsey asked. "What are you doing?"

"I'm fine," Marty replied.

"Where are you?"

"Out by the airport"

Expecting questions about what he was doing, he was surprised to hear, "Are you wearing the long-sleeved shirt that I bought you?" and, "Why didn't you call me today?"

"I was busy all day," Marty replied.

"Don't forget to call tomorrow. Take care, remember I love you," Betsey said.

By the time that Marty got off the phone, Don was asleep under the stars on the seat opposite Marty, and Tanisha had gone inside. Marty made himself a pillow out of his sweater and lay down in the cockpit opposite Don.

But he couldn't sleep. Don was snoring and competing with the noise of the aircraft taking off. He was thinking about how the goslings would be killed if they were captured. He kept going over what Tanisha had told him. Was it true that goslings would die instantly if their necks were squeezed? He remembered Pink, Puff, and Pickle and the three unnamed goslings that he had raised in his apartment. Before they grew up, they were cute feather-balls. How could anyone be so cruel as to dislocate the spine from the brain of a gosling?

Hearing dull thumps against the hull of his boat, he looked over the side and saw that geese were swimming alongside it. They were pecking at the boat, maybe trying to eat it. There were a lot of them. The geese from the beach had taken to the water. He remembered that geese liked the safety of calm water when they molt and that the bay by the airport was the calmest piece of water in Jamaica Bay.

Looking again, he saw that they were low in the water, not buoyed by their feathers, and he noticed that they had the same smell as chickens. The raft of geese was feeding. They moved in groups, calling each other when they found food.

Tanisha was also up. She was now used to the noise of aircraft taking off and was sleeping through it, but the dull thuds against the hull were new, and for a moment they scared her. She joined Marty looking over the side of the boat.

"When birds molt, they use a lot of energy to grow their new feathers. They are eating like crazy. They are preening a lot, and they seem grumpy. Geese itch when they molt," she said.

Getting no response from Marty she continued, "The geese will probably sleep on the water after feeding. They will post lookouts for predators."

Tanisha then gave Marty a tap on the shoulder, wished Marty goodnight, and went back into the cabin to sleep.

Marty had learned more about geese and bonded a little with Tanisha, but when he put his head down, he still could not sleep. His mind kept switching between Puff and Pink and Pickle and his plan for the next day. Hoping that it would make him sleepy, he took one of Don's beers. It was hot out; the beer helped a little. He wished that he could join the geese with a nighttime swim, but the water in this part of the bay was stagnant and dirty, and not far away was the dead zone he was familiar with. Marty was irritable, hungry, and hot as he fell into a fitful sleep.

Behold Goose!

"The other thing is that in the morning, they are flocked tight, and so it's easier to round them up." —Lee Humberg, Biologist, New York Magazine, Summer 2011.

The next morning, the roundup began again near the gate in the airport fence. Not wanting to make their presence known, Tanisha, Don, and Marty headed for an area about 200 yards west of the gate. This area had pebbles and rocks on the beach and was overgrown. There was a band of grass and reeds between the beach and the airport fence.

Marty crouched down to observe the roundup. There were five Department of Agriculture Wildlife Services guys, including Bill Bruford and his sidekick Donny, a National Parks Services guy (the Smokey), and two security guards. One of the security guards looked to be from Ace Security and the other was Port Authority Police. Lee Humberg, the biologist, was at the rear. The Smokey stood out from the rest with his short-sleeved fawn shirt and green pants, which contrasted with his sunburnt ears. Bill Bruford was wearing a short-sleeved white shirt, sunglasses, and a baseball cap, he was nicely suntanned, with a reddish glow to his face and arms.

By contrast, Marty, and Tanisha still had yesterday's clothes on. But Don had replaced his Hawaiian shirt with a subdued blue top.

"It looks like the Smokey is showing off the park service uniform despite the cold. Do you remember the Ace Guard that we saw when you were cutting holes in the crates? I think it's the same guy. Remember his limp?" Tanisha said.

"I can't see them clearly from this distance, but I remember that there were four red balls on the Ace Security badge," Marty replied.

"Bill Bruford seems to be in charge of the group. He's talking into a walkie-talkie, and the Port Authority Policeman is carrying a camera. I hope he's not taking photos," said Tanisha.

The Wildlife Services guys were busy. Two of them were in kayaks, guiding the geese towards the shore. Donny and another guy were standing by the corral netting and the pen and were wearing gloves. It looked like they were getting ready to crate the geese. Bruford, himself, didn't seem to have a job and stood talking to the Smokey. Marty noticed that the geese seemed to sense danger but weren't taking flight, they were probably in full molt and unable to fly. Inland on the dirt road that led to the airport gate, there was a truck with orange crates on it.

Away from the group, Lee Humberg, the biologist, appeared to be collecting samples. But samples of what? He had scissors, a marker, and plastic bags. He could be collecting anything from goose droppings to plant life.

"It's going to be really difficult to stop this. They are organized and we are outnumbered," said Marty after he had watched the goings-on for several minutes.

"If we could get the geese to come over here it would make it harder for them to corral them. Here it's rocky and overgrown near the fence. There is also no road back to the airport from here," Tanisha replied.

"Why are the geese not putting up a fight?" Marty asked.

"They are probably resident Canada geese and they don't see people as enemies. I can't be sure though, as they are molting and it's hard to identify them," Tanisha replied.

"So, what are they afraid of?"

"Their enemies are dogs, foxes, coyotes, and eagles."

"We can't call them over. They have no wing feathers. They can't fly."

"They can paddle over. If we can get them over here, they stand a chance."

"They have already caged some of the geese. Do you hear the bleating coming from the crate on the truck?"

"Call the geese," Tanisha said.

Marty thought for a moment, he had his Duck Commander with him, but if he called the geese, this would get the attention of Bruford and his team. But there was nothing to lose.

"I'll float out my duck decoy first," Marty said.

"Your duck decoy has feathers painted on it. It does not look like a molting duck,"` Tanisha said.

Marty took out his Duck Commander and called "WI-CH, WI-CH, WI-CH, WI-CH, WI-CH," and two geese started to slowly paddle over.

"WI-CH, WI-CH, WI-CH, WI-CH, WI-CH," Marty called again.

"Can't you make a more natural sound? You are too loud. The geese can still hear you if you quiet down," Tanisha said.

Three more geese started to swim over followed by two goslings.

"WI-CH, WI-CH, WI-CH, WI-CH, WI-CH," Marty called again.

"Put your head down. The Smokey is looking over here," Tanisha said.

"Feed them when they get here. They will make a feeding sound, which will attract more geese," Marty said.

Tanisha pulled out several homemade corn-and-spinach puddings from her backpack. The puddings also included eggs, and they floated with the help of a block of Styrofoam. She pushed them out into the water.

Marty continued to call.

"The geese look really strange when they are bald. They look like balls of floating fat," Tanisha said as the geese got nearer.

Marty crept a little closer to take a look.

"Can you start to call?" Marty asked Don.

"WO-ACK, WO-ACK, WO-ACK, WO-ACK, WO-ACK," Don's first call was more of a series of honks, and by now the geese were paddling over in a group.

Don's second call was again a series of honks, "WO-ACK, WO-ACK, WO-ACK, WO-ACK, WO-ACK," and now a second group of geese was paddling and catching up with the first group, which had slowed.

The first group of geese closed in on the beach.

Marty noticed Bruford first, "They are coming over. Bill Bruford and Donny are heading our way. They have separated from the rest of the group," he said.

"They will see the boat when they get closer. There is nowhere to hide it," Tanisha said.

"If they ask what we are doing, we can tell them that we are hunting ducks," said Marty.

"Why lie?" Tanisha asked.

"Duck hunters don't threaten them," Marty replied.

But Bill Bruford didn't ask. "This area is closed," he shouted from a distance.

"What's happening?" Marty asked.

"We're rounding up geese," Bill Bruford replied.

"Why?" Marty asked.

"They're a danger to airplanes. Didn't you hear about the plane that landed on the Hudson after it collided with geese. Did you put the corn in the water?"

Bill Bruford then came up close to Marty. So close, that Marty could see his abs showing through his white shirt. Marty thought back to the picture he had of Bruford and the little league team, Bruford looked like a little league coach. One who coached a bunch of clean-cut blond kids who were keen on the game.

"We fed them to encourage them to stay."

"This area is closed."

"Do you mind if Don shoots a few geese?" Marty asked, pointing to Don.

"Why?"

"I'd like to roast one."

"Don can shoot as many geese as he wants. They are on their way to be gassed."

Tanisha glared at Marty, and Marty felt her anger.

"Who is she?" asked Bruford.

"She's squeamish," Marty replied.

"Look, I have changed my mind. I can't have pellets in the geese. The geese are going to a poultry processing plant. Someone could eat a goose with a pellet in it and crack a tooth."

Marty pushed down the muzzle of the gun that was under Don's arm "Just one, we'll carry out the body," he said.

Tanisha glared again.

"Does he have a license to shoot geese?" Bill Bruford asked.

"Don, show him your federal duck stamp," Marty said.

Don took the stamp out of his wallet and showed it to Bruford.

"Just one and make it quick," Bill Bruford said.

Don broke open his shotgun and removed the cartridge. He then visually checked the gun and loaded a longer shell.

"I prefer the power of the three-and-a half-inch-shell and the number two shot when I'm shooting geese," Don observed.

Bruford then pressed talk on his walkie-talkie radio, "Bill to team, come in," he said. The radio crackled before Bill continued, "Bring the corral netting, the pens, and crates over here."

Marty stepped back from Bruford and Tanisha and Don followed. They were off the beach, on the grass, almost as far inland as the reeds. The reeds were more yellow than green, it was a yellow-green that Marty liked, but there was no time to observe.

"What the hell are you doing, helping Wildlife Services?" Tanisha asked.

"If Don shoots a goose it might set off the rest of the geese," Marty replied.

"And…" Tanisha asked.

"Do you remember when we were at the Jamaica Bay Wildlife Center and I went too close to the gosling and the goose charged me? Geese can be aggressive if they are provoked," Marty said.

"Can I shoot one?" Don asked.

"Hold off, I need to figure out which one," Marty whispered to Don.

"Get a move on," Bill Bruford shouted.

And Don looked in Bill Bruford's direction until Marty, feeling scared that this would go wrong, pulled Don around.

"Watch the geese. Watch the geese. Don't watch Bill Bruford," said Marty.

Marty had noticed the gander on patrol. To the left of the gander was a smaller goose, which Marty took to be the female. To the left of the female there were two goslings. A complete goose family.

"We've got to get the gander to fight," Marty said to Tanisha. Pointing to the left of the gander, Marty asked Tanisha, "Should Don shoot the female or the goslings?"

"The goslings, they protect their young, but Don sometimes misses."

"The geese are not moving. They are only 20 feet away. Don has a front sight on his gun. He only has to line the gun up."

Marty couldn't bring himself to ask Don to shoot a gosling, "Shoot the female next to the gander and then move to put Bill Bruford between yourself and the gander," he said to Don.

Don signaled his intention to shoot to Bruford, shouldered the gun, and then bent his front knee while straightening his rear leg. He then looked down the barrel of the shotgun and aimed at the female. There was a bang and then feathers flew as the heavy shot peppered the head of the female goose. The goose shuddered, went a few feet in the air in the direction of the shot, and landed on the beach.

There were cries of pain and confusion among the geese. The geese on the beach ran in all directions. The geese on the water paddled away. The gander, however, turned and stood his ground. He bent his neck back slightly and then started to pump its head up and down. He then hissed, flapped his wings, and charged at Don, almost becoming airborne in the process. But Don ducked behind Bill Bruford and the gander turned towards Bruford. Bill Bruford clipped his walkie-talkie to his belt and tried to grab the gander with both hands.

Don made a move as if to come to Bruford's help.

"Let me handle this," Bruford said.

Marty, wondering if this could go any better, stepped back from the beach into a gap in the reeds, as did Bruford's sidekick Donny.

"Don't hurt the gander," Tanisha said.

"Stay away," Bruford replied.

Bruford made another grab for the goose and caught it by the wing. The goose looked like it weighed 20 pounds, and its wings were huge.

The gander squealed and all the geese turned to look. The ones on land turned quickly, the ones on the water had to paddle around. The gander went for Bruford with its beak and he tried to hold the gander at arm's length, but his arms were not long enough. He looked to be in pain as he started to head back towards the crates at the gate. But to get there, he had to pass the geese on the beach. They hissed and splayed their bald wings. Mud flew in all directions. Bill Bruford managed to beat off two of them, but then two more attacked. They had Bill Bruford outnumbered, 20 or 30 to one.

Marty could see Bill Bruford's anger building. His eyes were glaring. His jaw muscles tightened. There was also blood running down his right arm. He should not have grabbed the goose by the wing. Bruford clenched his teeth and the veins on his forehead enlarged.

In a final move to get away, Bill Bruford released the gander, dropped his walkie-talkie, and picked up a piece of driftwood to swipe at the attacking geese. He cleared an area around himself and then swung the driftwood at any goose that came near. By now, mud had covered his white shirt and his cap was gone; his pants and his boots were also muddy. Still wielding the wood, he retreated slowly back towards his colleagues, leaving Donny behind.

There was no obvious victory, yet it was over. The geese had won the battle in the first act. But did they understand this? Did they know that they were now safe? (Well, safe at least for today.) The birds that had been compliant and meek now spaced themselves out a few feet apart, their feet were slightly apart and the necks were out. The atmosphere had changed, they no longer picked at weeds, they were on guard.

Marty couldn't figure why the rest of the team hadn't come to help Bruford until he remembered that Bill Bruford was a loner, and without orders, the team was not going to come to his help. What had Betsey said? Study the enemy. Maybe he'd followed her directions subconsciously.

Marty also looked over towards the gate, thinking about the geese that were already in crates, which were still on the truck. Unless Bruford canceled this roundup and let them go, they were on their way to be gassed.

A bit later, Tanisha pointed out to Marty that the gander was injured and that another goose had taken his place as a lookout. Marty remembered watching geese fly in a V formation and how they took turns to lead. When the leader tires, he falls back and another bird comes forward to break the wind. Bill Bruford was out of action, but nobody had taken his place. The Wildlife Services team had not studied geese in flight.

Two geese were sticking by the injured gander, "What's going on?" Marty asked Tanisha.

"Geese take care of their injured," Tanisha replied. Tanisha then took Marty by the arm and said, "Your crazy ideas are starting to make sense. Do you remember when you destroyed the crates by the airport? At the time, it made no sense. Same thing with shooting the goose, I thought that you were out of your mind. But shooting the one goose saved the flock."

Marty, though, knew different. He hadn't had a plan two years ago when he cut holes in the crates, and his recent success was due to his new girlfriend. It was Betsey who had told him to study the enemy.

On the trip back on the beach towards the airport gate, Marty opened a can of beer. He drank it quickly and tossed the can in the water and waited for Tanisha to complain about litter. There was no complaint, only a smile.

Only the dead goose in the blanket that Tanisha was carrying on her shoulder dampened the mood. It had not bled out, but it oozed a clear, sticky liquid that seeped through the cloth and onto her shirt.

"Do you think that the gander will find another mate?" Marty asked.

Tanisha stroked the dead goose, "It might not find another mate. Geese mate for life," she replied.

The Journey Home

As Tanisha stepped into the water to go out to Mart's boat the gander, the injured mate of the dead goose, followed her. Stepping onto the boat she put the dead goose inside the cabin and then came out and sat down opposite Don and Marty.

Don's inflatable had an engine problem and he had no choice but to return to Dead Horse Bay with Tanisha and Marty and get a mechanic. Don didn't want to return with Marty, as the last time he'd traveled with Marty, Marty's boat heeled a lot.

As Marty set sail, he looked around to see if the injured gander was still following them. It was afloat just off the beach, not swimming, as if it were trying to make up its mind whether to follow or not. Unlike yesterday, the gander was calm and feeding, looking around as if it were expecting another goose to join him. Maybe it could smell its dead mate. After a bit, it noticed Marty's boat, and as the boat picked up speed, the gander stretched out its long neck flat on the water and swam after it. It followed the boat closely as it left Grassy Bay on its way to Duck Creek Marsh, a small salt marsh island, just offshore. The gander almost caught up with the boat as they drew parallel to Duck Creek Marsh.

"Why is the gander following us?" Marty asked.

"He might know that we have his mate with us," Tanisha replied.

"How?" asked Marty.

"I don't know. Maybe he saw me wrap the female in the blanket, or maybe he can follow the smell. He has very good eyesight. It sees more than 180 degrees horizontally and vertically," Tanisha replied.

"I'm going to lose him."

"Why?"

"Otherwise, he will follow us all the way back to Dead Horse Bay."

The gander fell out of sight momentarily as Marty ducked behind the marsh into Hassock Creek. It then reappeared behind them. Seeing him, Marty turned again, making a sharper turn, but again the goose reappeared behind them. Marty, figuring that this was a silly game, gave up trying to lose the gander, but he didn't tell Tanisha that he had given up. He knew that his failure would amuse her. He passed the low-lying islands of East High Meadows, Winhole Point, and Winhole Hassock before he reached the deep waters of Winhole Channel.

Relaxing, Marty looked in Tanisha's direction, Tanisha laughed as though she knew about his failed attempt to lose the goose. Just for a moment, her eyes sparkled and her hair shone. The smile was kind. Marty noticed that she had removed her makeup and somehow managed to find a change of clothes. Looking away from Tanisha, Don looked the same as he did two days back when they had come out to the airport. Don hadn't changed his clothes or groomed his beard.

"I'm beat. I couldn't sleep last night because of the airplane noise. I'm going to take a nap. Can you wake me when we get back?" Tanisha asked Marty.

"Yes," Marty replied.

As she was climbing down into the boat's cabin, she called back, "Marty."

"What?" Marty replied.

"Can you move the goose from the cabin floor?" Tanisha asked.

"Yes," Marty replied.

Tanisha handed Marty the goose, which Marty lowered carefully into the cockpit locker.

With Tanisha out of sight, Don asked, "Why are we taking the dead goose with us?"

"She wants to bury it," Marty replied.

"Can't we lose it?" Don asked, "It smells and I don't want to be caught with a dead goose. It's not goose-hunting season."

"Tanisha says that the gander is a hero. She wants to give it a proper burial," Marty replied.

"Don't my wishes count?" Don asked, "You know that it was hard for me to shoot it."

"We'll keep it out of sight. We will be back at the marina soon."

Don looked miffed at Marty's reply, so Marty went back to sailing the boat.

As Marty entered Beach Channel, he realized that he would have to sail into the wind to get back. Confidently, he started tacking. Before each turn, he went as close inshore as he dared, and on the straight tacks he kept the boat on course by aiming it towards a mark onshore. He maintained as much speed as possible by tweaking the sails. And he tacked the boat himself, without asking Don for help. Marty was dancing a joyous, crazy, zig-zag waltz. Marty's concerns about the gander were gone.

The boat heeled heavily after the first tack, maybe 40 degrees. Don's weight was on the leeward side and along with the wind, it pushed the boat into the water.

As he went in close to the Brand Point Wildlife Sanctuary, Marty became curious. He looked inland, but there was nothing to see from the waterside.

At the Cross Bay Memorial Bridge, the channel narrowed and Marty cut his tack short, slowing as he came into the wind.

At 116th street on the Rockaways, he came in close to the dock at The Wharf Bar. There were two powerboats at the dock and the crews were drinking.

At the junction of Beach Channel and Runway Channel, he went into Runway Channel before tacking back into Beach Channel. He used Runway Channel to get a wider tack.

At the Gil Hodges Memorial Bridge, he again slowed but he picked up speed as he approached red buoy 20, where he turned away from the wind and towards the marina. This was the end of Marty's beat into the wind with its zig-zagging. Don stood up and put his hand on Marty's shoulder, and when Marty turned towards him, Don asked, "Did you enjoy your sail?"

"Yes, it was fun," Marty replied.

"You lost the gander a mile back," Don said.

"I'd forgotten about him," Marty replied.

"He almost caught you for a third time at Brand Point Wildlife Sanctuary, but when you turned, he headed towards the beach," Don said.

"Is Tanisha still asleep?"

"Yes."

Marty laughed, "I'm sorry she missed seeing the gander head for the beach. She laughed at me when I was trying to lose it."

On the last of the straights the water became shallow, and Marty steered a course to avoid running aground. Sure of his course, Marty looked up at the sail and the sky. The sun was high in the sky, it was about two P.M. Away from the sun, the sky was indigo with white clouds. He looked at the clouds—cirrocumulus stratiform—very small cirrocumulus clouds that covered a large part of the sky. There were spaces or rifts between the individual cloudlets that the indigo blue sky filled. To the edge of his view, the clouds fell away and as they moved, he gazed at the fluctuating tones of blue behind them. It was beautiful. The sky had fixed itself to the top of the boat's mast.

Passing between buoys nine and ten, Marty turned towards Dead Horse Bay and the marina. It was a weekday afternoon, and not many people were out on the dock.

Marty didn't ask Don for help with docking, and just after he tied up the boat, he went inside and gently shook Tanisha's arm, "We're back," he said.

Then, picking up the goose from the locker, Marty felt its stiffness as he bent it to clear the locker's lid. Avian rigor mortise was setting in. The goose was about four feet long, had a six-foot wingspan, and weighed about 15 pounds. Wrapped in a blanket as it was, the goose was awkward to carry as it slipped around inside. Marty could feel the goose's shape. The three toes fanning out from its webfoot felt strange, so he grabbed the neck near the head.

"Can you help?" he asked Don.

"If Tanisha will take my shotgun and my backpack," Don replied.

"I'll carry it," Tanisha replied.

Don handed his shotgun to Tanisha.

Marty then passed the goose from the boat to Don who was on the dock. They were a strange-looking group walking down the dock. Don was in front, holding the goose's feet. Marty came next, holding the goose's neck, and Tanisha made up the rear, carrying Don's shotgun.

Don and Marty started the awkward walk up the dock, carrying the goose on their shoulders.

The Funeral

Marty and Don were carrying the goose up the dock when it slipped out of the blanket and fell to the dock.

A guy walking in the opposite direction asked, "Been fishing?"

Marty did not reply.

Tanisha, who was carrying Don's shotgun, stared at the guy.

Marty picked up the goose as the guy stared back.

"What are we going to do with it?" Marty asked as he held the goose.

"Bury it," Tanisha replied.

"We should not waste it. There shouldn't be shot in the body. Don shot it in the head. We could butcher it and roast it," Marty said.

Tanisha looked horrified, "If you cook it, you've cooked your goose. Have a heart. I'll stop calling you a hypocrite if you agree to bury it," she replied.

"Put it in the dumpster at the marina. It looks miserable and it won't be good to eat," Don said.

"What about Don's wishes?" Marty asked, "He keeps saying that I ignore him."

"He's outnumbered two to one if you change your mind," Tanisha replied.

"Where can we bury it?" Marty asked.

"I don't know," Tanisha replied.

"Why don't we bury it on the beach?" Marty said.

"In Dead Horse Bay among the junk?" Tanisha asked.

"We might be able to sell it on craigslist," Don said. And then he asked, "Did either of you try to find out where the goose came from? We could mail in the ring on its neck and find out where it was ringed. We might find the place that it had visited the most and bury it there."

"That would take time, and we have nowhere to store it. It's four foot long, and its wingspan is six foot. It's not going to fit in my fridge," Marty replied.

"So, we're agreed. We're going to bury the goose on the beach at Dead Horse Bay," Tanisha said.

Don took hold of the goose's feet and again wrapped it in the blanket as they continued up the dock.

Marty and Don slowed at the end of the dock before continuing up the ramp. They passed the blue sheds of Buster's Marine and continued into the car park, past the marina's dumpster and the picnic area, and then turned towards the water. They scrambled down the drop that led to the beach. At this point, Marty realized that someone was following them, as Cathy, who worked at Buster's Marine, came up behind him and took his shoulder.

"I know what you are you up to." said Cathy, who was carrying an old camera around her neck.

"You seem to know about everything that goes on here," Marty replied.

"I told you that you should help her," Cathy said.

"I started to like geese. They get a bad rap. I wasn't just helping Tanisha," replied Marty.

"You always did like them. Do you remember how you went off cats when I told you that they ate goslings?" said Cathy.

"I just didn't like the idea of goslings being eaten," Marty replied.

"Can I see inside the blanket?" Cathy asked.

Marty, opened the blanket with the goose so that she could look, "Burying a goose," he said.

"I've had a lot of experience burying relatives."

"Yes, but not geese," Marty felt a warmth coming to his face. His face was blotchy and red, and now warm, yet his smile did not disappear.

Moving onto the beach, the wind smelled of mildew and dead shellfish. Someone had set up a line of glass bottles on a piece of driftwood, a variety of colors and shapes, artfully arranged and evenly spaced. The sun shone through one of the bottles and Marty wanted to put it in his pocket, but he left it where it was. The bottle looked pretty on the beach

Marty then located a burial spot in the wet sand below the lines of washed-up straw that marked the recent high tides.

Marty smiled quickly at Cathy and then his face straightened. He said, "We can bury her here in the clean sand between the two lines of straw. The goose would be in the water some of the day and out of the water the rest, like she was when she was alive. It should not be hard to dig a hole in the sand,"

Along the shore, there was a 20-foot strip of glass, pebbles, garbage, and shells. Then, going inland, there was a strip of clean sand, then a line of straw, then another strip of clean sand, and then another line of straw followed by dry sand that went all the way inshore. Recent high tides had washed up lines of straw and shells, but the glass and garbage had been washed out of the landfill.

Marty placed the goose on the beach with its feet pointing towards the water, and with his finger he drew a line around the goose. Then after moving the goose aside he started to dig a shallow grave using the butt of Don's shotgun to move the sand. He uncovered a couple of mud-filled glass bottles, which he examined and put aside. A large, brown glass bottle was round and half-filled with sand, it was maybe 18 inches long, and a small bottle was clear and rectangular. The large bottle was home to a small crab and the small bottle had grass growing inside it. He also uncovered a sawn horse bone with a hole in the center where the marrow had been, a reminder of the glue factories that operated here in the 1940s. This he held up for everyone to see. Most of everything he uncovered was either chipped, broken, or rusting away.

Some ten minutes later he'd finished digging the shallow grave, which had an outline that looked like a misshapen snow angel.

It was a quiet moment. Marty could hear the lapping waves, and he could also hear a clear ringing sound, the whispering sound of water moving through the broken bottles on the glass-strewn beach.

Marty then laid the goose in the hole. It looked pale and thin with a particularly scrawny neck. The goose was sharp to the touch where the new quills were coming in, and he felt the pricks.

Cathy took a picture of the scene with the goose and Marty, Don, and Tanisha before Marty started to cover the goose with sand.

"We could cover the grave with horseshoe crab shells and a few stones. There are a lot of horseshoe crab shells washed up on the beach," Tanisha said.

"Crabs and geese," Marty replied.

"This is way too serious. Why do Canada geese cries sometimes sound like WAH, WAH instead of WO-ACK, WO-ACK?" Don said.

"Why?" Marty replied.

"Because they're frickin' Canadian," Don said.

Next, Marty placed what they thought could have been the goose's three favorite things into the grave: a corn-and-spinach pudding, her goose tag, and a picture of a gander. Marty didn't have an actual picture of her mate; the picture was symbolic.

Marty read the eulogy.

"We commit to almighty God this beautiful creature that gave its life so that the other creatures might live. This goose traveled south in the bitter cold of winter and died during the summer molt of 2012. This once-beautiful and graceful goose, this scrawny, fatty, molting goose died to save the lives of hundreds of geese gathered at Kennedy Airport," said Marty.

After this came Don's one-shot salute from his single-shot 12-gauge shotgun.

Marty and Tanisha then started to cover the goose with sand while Don stood by holding his shotgun at a respectable angle on his shoulder. Marty then placed a large stone as a marker on the grave and placed horseshoe crab shells around the edge. Picking up one of the horseshoe crab shells, Marty touched its long-pointed tail and its helmet-shaped body. Turning it over carefully, he looked at its old dead eyes and then put it back down on the sand.

There was only one other person on the beach, a woman at the far end. Her face was indistinguishable in the distance. Even so, Marty wished that she weren't there. He wanted the space to himself. He didn't care for the bright orange jacket that she was wearing.

By the time that they left the burial, tears filled Tanisha's eyes. Marty felt cold and disoriented, and Don had respectfully put his shotgun back on his shoulder. Not wanting to go home directly, they walked slowly back to the trail that led down to the beach.

Marty's Arrest

A photograph is supposed not to evoke but to show. That is why photographs, unlike handmade images, can count as evidence. But evidence of what?
—Susan Sontag

Tuesday afternoon, two days after the goose's funeral, Marty was still feeling happy about the rescue when his doorbell rang. At the door were two uniformed policemen, a sergeant and an officer. They had a warrant for his arrest, and worse, the sergeant smiled as he handcuffed Marty and bundled him into the back of the police car.

Marty's view during the ride to the precinct was the back of the policemen's heads. He took his time to observe them. The sergeant was driving and he was at least six inches taller than the officer, who was short and bald. They were both red-necked and at some point, the sergeant had worn glasses. You could see the white outline on the side of his head where the glasses frames shielded his skin from the sun.

Parking in front of the precinct, the officer turned around and said, "Our orders were to pick you up."

"Why?" asked Marty.

"The Port Authority Police said that you trespassed at Kennedy Airport. They also said that you had interfered with the roundup of geese," replied the officer.

The officer then got out of the car and opened the back door for Marty, took Marty's arm, and led him inside the station. He led Marty to a desk in an open area and told him to sit down. The officer sat at the desk and leaned into it and towards Marty as he flipped through papers.

The sergeant appeared a little later, saying, "He's not going to run. Can I get my cuffs back?"

"Sure," the officer replied.

The sergeant uncuffed Marty.

"Put him in the holding cell until the detectives get back?" asked the sergeant.

"Who wants to talk to him?"

"Prentice."

Hearing the sergeant say the name of the detective, Marty almost asked for the sergeant's name. But, thinking that this might appear as a belligerent move, he decided against it.

"Is there any evidence?" asked the officer.

"Prentice has a photo," said the sergeant.

"When can I leave?" asked Marty.

"We're just uniform, ask the detective," replied the officer.

He then motioned for Marty to get up and follow him down a corridor to a holding cell.

The holding cell was small, about six feet by eight feet, with brick walls and a steel door that had a small glass window. There was a vent in the left wall with a fan and maybe air-conditioning. There was a steel bedstead anchored to the floor, a mattress, and a one-piece metal sink and toilet at the far end of the room. The mattress had a green cover, it looked attractive but when Marty felt it, he knew that it would be uncomfortable.

Marty paced a little, peered out of the small glass window, and then laid on his back on the bed and stared at the ceiling. He had time to think, although his thoughts didn't seem to follow any logical pattern.

Had Tanisha and Don also been arrested? Why hadn't he been read his Miranda rights? How had the police found him? How long would they keep him? Would he be able to get out on bail? Would he get the chance to make a phone call? And if he did, who would he call? And why had they arrested him now? He'd been out to the airport several times and had not been under arrest before.

There were no answers, but it was too noisy to nap.

Everything in the police station was loud. The police were down the corridor from his cell, and he could hear their greetings as they came and went. The precinct door slammed open and shut. He could hear car horns through the cell walls. And if he listened carefully, he could hear the conversation on a police radio and the whine from the fan and the air-conditioning.

He'd been in the holding cell for six hours when the cell door opened. The arresting officer reappeared and took him out of the cell. Then, back through the open area, to another corridor and another interview room. In the interrogation room, two men sat at a metal table. Marty assumed that one of them was detective Prentice. Marty stood until the officer motioned for him to sit at the table.

Prentice introduced himself, saying "I'm detective Prentice and this is sergeant Oswald."

Prentice wore a faded-orange t-shirt and blue jeans while Oswald wore an open-neck shirt and khakis. They were maybe 40 years old, medium build, and about the same height, five-foot-six, maybe five-foot-eight. Oswald was on the wrong side of handsome. It wasn't his body that was responsible for this, but he had a misshaped head. Prentice would have been good-looking if he had taken the trouble to dress carefully.

It was detective Prentice who did most of the talking. He started by asking, "Did you take your boat out to Kennedy Airport?"

"Yes, officer," Marty replied.

"Do you know that there is a Maritime Security Zone around the airport?" Prentice continued.

"Yes, it's 100 yards. I anchored my boat outside it," replied Marty.

"Where is your boat now?" asked Prentice.

"At the marina at Dead Horse Bay," replied Marty.

"But you did take it to the airport?"

"Yes," replied Marty as he looked around the room. It was a plain room with spartan furniture, a tape recorder that appeared to be off, four metal chairs, and a metal table. The table sat in the middle of the room on the only soft furnishing was a worn blue rug.

"I have a photo of you on the beach," said Prentice as he handed the photo to Marty, "They say that you interfered with a goose roundup and that you shot a goose."

Marty looked carefully at the photo, "Can I keep it?" he asked.

"Why?"

"I'd like to study it."

"Keep it," said Prentice.

"Who is the guy in the photo with his back to the camera?" asked Prentice.

Marty recognized Don, but replied, "I can't see his face."

Prentice then asked, "Did you interfere with the goose roundup?"

"No," Marty replied.

"That's not what they say."

"I asked Bill Bruford if my friend could shoot a goose. I told Bruford that I wanted a goose to cook."

"And?"

"Bruford said that we could shoot as many geese as we wanted, as they were all going to be gassed. But when we shot the one goose, the other geese went mad, they went crazy, they first attacked my friend, and then they attacked Bruford."

"Who is Bruford?"

"He's a supervisor, he works for The United States Department of Agriculture Wildlife Services, the USDA."

"What did you do with the dead goose?"

"We brought it back to Dead Horse Bay."

"Did you cook it?"

"I wanted to cook it, but my friend said that the goose was a hero and that its death had saved the life of the geese in the flock and that it should have a hero's burial."

"What's the name of your friend?"

"I'd rather not say."

"And the Port Authority cop who was with Bruford, why didn't he help Bruford when the geese attacked?"

"He might have wanted overtime pay," Marty replied.

Marty knew that the New York Police Department was jealous of the hundreds of hours of overtime that the Port Authority Police got policing the airport. The NYPD felt that they were entitled to the same overtime. Marty, somehow, felt that this might be useful knowledge.

When Prentice didn't respond to his overtime comment Marty continued, "I'm sure that, if you had been there, you would have helped."

"You're right there," Prenticed said.

Marty couldn't read Prentice. He appeared not to react to what Marty had said about overtime, but sergeant Oswald had smiled. Oswald's mood might be changing, he might be softening.

Prentice then whispered to Oswald and the two of them left the interrogation room. They returned with coffee a few minutes later. They weren't talking when they returned, but Prentice looked mad and Marty guessed that they had argued. Marty hoped that Oswald, who had senior rank, would get his way.

Oswald sat down on the desk and Prentice stood nearby.

Prentice looked down at Oswald and said, "I'm surprised that you didn't get him a coffee."

Oswald ignored this but asked Marty, "Were you ever asked to leave the beach by the airport?"

"No," Marty replied.

"Does he have any priors?" Oswald asked Prentice.

"No," Prentice replied.

"Can I see your driver's license?" Oswald asked.

"You have my wallet. You took it from me when you brought me into the station," replied Marty.

"What about the girl that was with him?" asked Oswald.

"She's clean. She's a student at Brooklyn Law," replied Prentice.

"I'm going to send you home," Oswald said.

Marty was surprised, he was expecting to spend more time at the precinct and to be charged. He was going to say this but thought better of it. They might keep him longer if he expressed his surprise.

"I'm releasing you on a desk appearance ticket," said Oswald.

"What's that?" asked Marty, as he became aware that he was not getting off.

"In two weeks, you have to turn up in court with the ticket. In court, you will be arraigned. I'd advise you to turn up with a lawyer," said Oswald.

Marty had been at the precinct for eight hours before he was released. It was dark out now and the streets were deserted. On the street, his arrest preoccupied him, and he took a wrong turn, which took him through a neighborhood that he was not familiar with. He felt for his phone and a map, but the phone wasn't in his pocket. He'd probably not picked it up from his table when the police came to his door. Then he took another wrong turn and stood still long enough to focus. It took a while for him to stop thinking about his arrest and concentrate on getting home.

When he got home, but before he went to bed, Marty looked at the desk appearance ticket. The ticket said that he had to appear at Brooklyn Criminal Court. The offense was listed as §140: Trespass. The ticket had a docket number, a date and time for the court appearance, and the court address. Marty had expected the court to be in Queens, as Kennedy was in Queens and it was there that he'd been photographed helping geese.

The Coffee Shop

Marty got only sketchy details of Tanisha's arrest when he phoned her. She wanted to meet in person, not talk on the phone. He agreed to meet her at a coffee shop near her college.

When Marty got there, he was anxious to discuss her experience with the cops. But when he met her, the first thing he noticed was that she was wearing a dress and, if he was correct, makeup. This wasn't the Tanisha that he knew; she usually wore pants, a sleeveless shirt, and a big smile.

Tanisha noticed Marty looking at her dress, "I was talking to a lawyer last night. He said it would help if I looked professional," she said.

"Are you wearing makeup?" Marty asked.

"Yes, I'm trying to look good in the dress," Tanisha replied.

They took a table away from the door, and Marty went to the counter to get coffee. Returning, he saw that Tanisha's chair was empty, but her bag was on the table. She hadn't left, but where was she? Marty looked around, noticed the dark wood walls, the small stools with buttoned red seat cushions, the old wood, the tin ceiling, and the brass ashtrays screwed to the bar. Marty concluded that this shop hadn't always been a coffee shop, it had once sold liquor.

Marty heard a noise from the bathroom and then Tanisha reappeared.

"Who is the lawyer?" Marty asked.

"He's my legal history lecturer. But can we talk about the arrests?" asked Tanisha.

"You wouldn't talk yesterday," said Marty.

"I didn't want to talk on the phone," replied Tanisha.

"How long did they keep you?" Marty asked.

"Overnight," replied Tanisha.

"Why?"

"I insisted on calling my dad, and the cops took forever to get me a phone."

"Is your dad going to help?"

"He offered to get me a lawyer, but I just wanted him to know that I was safe. When I called him from the police station, someone was listening in on the call, I could hear breathing, and it wasn't my dad."

"Are you sure?"

"Yes."

"I see now why you don't want to talk on the phone."

"I have to be careful," said Tanisha.

"Was your dad mad when he found out that you were in trouble?" asked Marty.

"We don't get on, but when I'm in trouble he's on my side."

"Did they try to get you to confess?"

"No, I don't think they were looking for a confession. They have a photo of us out by the airport. They seem to think that the photo proves that we were trespassing."

"It doesn't," replied Marty.

"They do want to nail us for something," said Tanisha.

"I'm not working. It wouldn't be a disaster if I had to spend a little time in jail."

"I'm in law school, I can't practice law if I get a criminal record."

Marty fell silent, drank more coffee, and then went back to the counter to get the plain round pastry that he'd noticed. He then picked up a copy of *Book Forum* from the bookshelf behind his seat and scanned the contents page. It was the least literary of the literary magazines that the coffee shop made available for customers, but it was still too dense for Marty. He'd have liked a distraction, but the bookshelf had issues of *The New York Review of Books*, *Book Forum*, and *The London Review of Books*. In the meantime, Tanisha began to fiddle with her cell phone.

Putting her phone back in her bag Tanisha said, "You know, they kept asking me why a female law student was out by the airport. They didn't believe me when I told them that I was rescuing geese. I told them to stop with the microaggression. But you know, I don't think they understood microaggression. I also don't think they know that you had cut holes in the turkey crates. They would have complained if they had."

Marty had also noticed that the police did not ask about the holed turkey crates. He was happy about this, but he didn't want to talk about it with Tanisha, as she had warned him not to cut holes in the crates. He'd exhausted the arrest topic, so he asked, "Why did you decide to look for a lawyer?"

"Well, my dad said that I needed one. Then I remembered that one of my lecturers had turned up late for class and told the class that he'd been delayed at Brooklyn Criminal Court," replied Tanisha.

"So…" asked Marty.

"One of the girls in the class asked him why he'd been in court and he said that he'd been defending a student," said Tanisha.

"What's the lawyer's name?"

"Martin Quigley."

"What's he like?"

"He's liberal, the student he defended got arrested at a demo."

"What will he cost?" asked Marty.

"He offered to help us for free," replied Tanisha.

"Can I meet him?" asked Marty.

"He's going to meet us at the arraignment," replied Tanisha.

"Have you been in touch with Don?" asked Marty.

"No," replied Tanisha.

"I called him this morning. He wasn't arrested, and he didn't seem to have a care in the world. He was telling me about the tomatoes that he's grown."

"Lucky sod, his back is turned in the photo."

"He'll be in the courtroom."

"Why?"

"He's coming to support us."

"I'll slap him if he makes fun of me."

Tanisha's phone alerted her, and she took it out of her bag and showed Marty the text message. Marty saw that it was a petition from change.org. The liberal organization was circulating a petition for a group that wanted to stop animal abuse on the Discovery Channel.

"Do you get these messages?" asked Tanisha.

"I don't," said Marty.

"I get them all the time," said Tanisha.

"Do you support them?" asked Marty

"Yes, of course," replied Tanisha, "I don't get why you never talk about the environment, climate change, the polar ice caps, polluted oceans, or starving children. You only seem to be interested in rescuing geese."

"I only get involved when I can do something," replied Marty.

"That makes sense," said Tanisha, "But why do you confuse ducks and geese?"

"There is a connection. Don't you remember the day when I met you? I had been feeding cats. Sally told me that the cats ate ducklings, and you were talking about saving geese," replied Marty.

Tanisha laughed so hard that she began to tear up. She then wiped her eyes on her dress sleeve. She had looked a little down and very professional when she came into the coffee shop, and now Marty was glad to see the laughter. The old Tanisha was back.

Although he didn't respond to petitions for help, Marty had grown. Since he'd known Tanisha, he looked at wildlife differently. He didn't just look for yellow warblers out in the woods by Jamaica Bay, he also noticed barn swallows and he was now on the lookout for willow flycatchers. He'd become more interested in Canada geese, particularly since he'd raised the goslings that had replaced the geese that were rounded up in Prospect Park. He'd also started to notice other waterfowl, including black ducks, mallards, gadwalls, and ruddy ducks. He didn't confuse ducks and geese.

Brooklyn Criminal Court

In the week leading up to the arraignment, Marty felt increasingly blasé about it. He felt free, liberated, and glad that he'd helped rescue the geese. The fears that he had first felt during his arrest were gone.

If the case did go to trial, he had a defense. His defense against the trespass charge was that he'd not set foot inside the airport. He had looked carefully at the photo of himself on the beach by the airport, he could easily make out the no trespassing sign on the fence, and he had not gone inside the fence. He could use the photo to defend himself. He'd also been careful to anchor his boat 100 yards offshore. True, he'd come in close to the shore to let Tanisha step off, but after she'd got off, he'd anchored 100 yards offshore. His defense for interfering with the roundup of geese was that he hadn't. He'd not called geese away from the corral netting and the animal pens, he'd called ducks. It wasn't his fault if the geese had responded to his duck calls. He'd also not fed the geese when they came over, he'd fed ducks. The geese had mistakenly eaten the duck puddings.

Marty's mood changed as he headed towards the Lower Criminal Court at 120 Schermerhorn Street. Rain was falling. The line of police cars parked outside the building identified it surely enough.

Marty sheltered in the building entrance. He shared the shelter with a muscular guard who was wearing a black t-shirt with "New York Criminal Court" printed on it in bold white letters. For Criminal Court, Marty had dressed carefully and somewhat conservatively in a blue pea coat and blue-gray trousers.

He'd not been waiting long when Don arrived. Marty greeted him with, "I thought that you had forgotten me."

"How have you been?" responded Don.

"I could be better, I spent a day in a holding cell," Marty replied.

A little later, Tanisha and Martin Quigley, the attorney, arrived. Tanisha looked smart in a green-patterned dress, and Quigley wore a dark suit. Quigley said a quick "good morning" and motioned for them to go inside, Marty and Don followed him and Tanisha into the building.

Once inside, they had to empty the contents of their pockets into trays to pass through security. There was also a body scan, and Marty cursed when he was sent through the scan twice, having at first forgotten to remove his belt.

Beyond the metal detectors, the entrance to the court had upscale but dated decor. The most striking feature was the large decorative brass panels that covered recesses and the brass handrails with elaborate finials. The inside walls were beige or cream-colored, and there were many varnished wooden doors along the corridors.

Once inside, Marty was a bit lost. Quigley, who led them through the crowd to the elevator, saved him.

On the way to the elevator, Quigley asked Don, "Who are you?"

"I'm Don. I was with them at the airport."

"Were you arrested?" asked Quigley.

"No."

"Then why are you here?"

"I came to support them."

Quigley smiled at Don as he said, "That's nice of you."

In the elevator, Marty asked Quigley, "Why isn't the arraignment in Queens? Kennedy airport is in Queens."

"You were arrested in Brooklyn. Arraignments always take place in the borough of the arrest," replied Quigley.

Exiting the elevator on the third floor, Quigley said, "We'll talk outside the courtroom before we go in. When we do go inside, whisper and stay at the back of the room. Don't approach the judge."

Sitting in the center of the bench outside Room 321, Quigley asked, "Can I see the desk appearance tickets?"

Marty and Tanisha handed them over.

Quigley read each ticket carefully before announcing, "They are the same." He then turned to Marty and Tanisha he said, "I'll ask the judge to arraign you together. Your desk appearance tickets list §140: Trespassing. Also, because it's trespassing, I'm going to try and get the judge to rule today."

Quigley then asked, "Were you trespassing?"

Marty pulled a photo out of his pocket, and said, "They took this photo of us at the airport. If you look at it carefully you can see the no trespassing sign on the fence. We didn't go inside the fence. We were not trespassing."

"Okay, not guilty to trespassing. What else did the police talk to you about?" asked Quigley.

"Interfering with the roundup of geese," replied Marty.

"Did you?" asked Quigley.

"No," answered Marty.

"Yes," answered Tanisha.

"Which is it to be?" asked Quigley.

Marty broke in, "Let me finish. I asked for permission before we shot the goose."

"Why did you shoot a goose?" asked Quigley.

"Don shot the goose. I said that I planned to roast it," replied Marty.

"This Don?" asked Quigley as he reached over and put his hand on Don.

"Yes," Marty replied.

"Tell the truth. The geese were going passively to their deaths. You shot the goose to make them angry," said Tanisha.

"Did you?" asked Quigley.

"Yes," replied Marty.

"So, you did interfere," said Quigley.

"Only a little bit, and they don't know that we interfered unless you tell them. They think that we wanted to roast a goose," replied Marty.

"I will have to tell the truth if I'm asked," said Quigley.

"When Don shot the goose, the rest of the geese got mad. The gander charged first at Don and then it charged at Bill Bruford. Bruford grabbed the goose and then all hell broke loose. The geese became aggressive and came to the rescue of the goose that Bruford had grabbed. It was the geese that stopped the roundup, not us," said Marty.

"Tanisha told me about Bruford, but this judge doesn't like a slick defense," said Quigley. "Your best defense is to plead guilty, at least to something. I'll plead not guilty, but that might have to change. Let's go in. Remember what I said about whispering, and staying at the back."

Marty expected to see a lot of people in the courtroom, but there were only nine. The judge was behind a large desk at the center at the back and looked like a regular family man. Two men stood facing him, one at the left, the other on the right. A few more people sat at the back of the court, perhaps also waiting to be arraigned.

"Who are the guys facing the judge?" Marty asked Quigley.

"The one on the left is the prosecutor and the one on the right is the defense lawyer," replied Quigley.

Marty, Tanisha, and Don joined the other people at the back of the courtroom and waited for their tickets to come up. When they heard their tickets being called, Quigley took the tickets, walked up to the judge, and started to talk to him. Marty could make out the rhythm of the speech but was too far away to make out what they were saying. Quigley looked confident, he looked to be talking fluently, using long sentences. The judge kept interrupting like he was trying to cut Quigley short.

Returning, Quigley turned to Tanisha and said, "He wants guilty pleas. If you plead guilty, you will each get community service and a $250 fine. It won't happen today; there will still have to be another meeting, a conference in the judge's office, but it's almost a done deal."

Marty was silent, the outcome wasn't too bad.

"I can't have a criminal record," Tanisha said.

"You won't have a criminal record, both charges are violations, misdemeanors, and I can make sure that your records are sealed," replied Quigley.

Marty, who was on a tight budget, asked, "Why $250?"

Quigley took out his phone and brought up Google Chrome, and when the result from his search came back, he read: "Section 261.3(c), Intentionally interfering with any Forest Service volunteer, enrollee, or employee in performance of duties, $250."

"We should pay. It won't prevent me from practicing law," said Tanisha who was smiling.

Quigley looked at Tanisha and said, "Stop smiling, the judge is looking this way. I don't want him to see that you are happy with the outcome until it's a done deal. Let me go back to the judge."

There was a long wait before Quigley returned. When he did get back, he turned to Tanisha and said, "It's done. You can smile. We still have to meet with the prosecutor and the judge next week, but it's a formality. We'll get the paperwork then. You'll both get two weeks of community service and a $250 fine."

"Thanks," Marty said to Quigley.

Tanisha stepped towards Quigley, got up on her heels, and hugged him.

Turning to Marty, Quigley said, "You got away with it. You were lucky that the police released you on a desk appearance ticket, and you did the right thing by agreeing to plead guilty."

Tanisha smiled again and waved at the judge.

"Let's get out of here and celebrate," said Marty.